**"We're not those people anymore— those people we once were."**

"But we are," Trent said. "We have their memories, their souls."

But not their hearts. At least not hers.

Alaina reached for Trent. This time he came to her, desire catching fire between them.

She was overwhelmed. "I can feel you…what you feel."

"I can feel you, too."

"You want me," she said. "So take me. I want to know what it was like between us."

Trent shuddered now. She knew him so well. And still she wanted him?

He took her in his arms. "This is your last chance," he warned her. "Your last chance to leave."

She shook her head. "You don't scare me."

"Then that makes one of us."

## Books by Lisa Childs

Harlequin Nocturne

*Haunted* #5
*Persecuted* #14
*Damned* #22
*Immortal Bride* #59
*Mistress of the Underground* #84
*Déjà Vu* #114

---

## LISA CHILDS

has been writing since she could first form sentences. At eleven, she won her first writing award and was interviewed by the local newspaper. That story's plot revolved around a kidnapping, probably something she wished on any of her six siblings. A Halloween birthday predestined a life of writing paranormal and intrigue. Readers can write to Lisa at PO Box 139, Marne, MI 49435 or visit her at her website www.lisachilds.com.

# DÉJÀ VU

## LISA CHILDS

TORONTO NEW YORK LONDON
AMSTERDAM PARIS SYDNEY HAMBURG
STOCKHOLM ATHENS TOKYO MILAN MADRID
PRAGUE WARSAW BUDAPEST AUCKLAND

Recycling programs
for this product may
not exist in your area.

ISBN-13: 978-0-373-61861-3

DÉJÀ VU

Copyright © 2011 by Lisa Childs-Theeuwes

Dear Reader,

Have you ever had a sense of déjà vu? I have.
Maybe it's just because I'm quite forgetful and
don't remember the first experience. But the
fanciful part of me would rather believe I really
have experienced it before—in another life.

FBI agent Alaina Paulsen has that sense of
déjà vu when she meets infamous horror author
Trent Baines. But she doesn't know if the man
was her lover in a previous life or her killer. She
remembers her past death, a murder so gruesome
that she still has a scar. The killer has also carried
over into this life, and he's determined to kill her
again.

I hope you enjoy reading about Alaina and Trent's
thrilling *Déjà Vu!*

Lisa Childs

With great appreciation
to Tara Gavin and Shawna Rice.
Thank you for everything!

# Prologue

*Light glinted off metal as a clenched fist lifted a knife high in the air. The blade flashed again as it descended, slicing through flesh until the point plunged deep into her heart. The fist withdrew the knife and blood gurgled out of the wound as her last breath gasped from her lungs.*

*"You'll stop loving him now," the man murmured as he wiped her blood from his knife.*

*She stared up at him, her eyes still wide with fear even as she died and her spirit left this body....*

\* \* \*

With the image so vivid in her mind, Alaina struggled to focus on the one in the mirror on the bathroom door. Her image. The steam blurred her features, so that she saw only blond hair and pale skin. She wiped a hand over the fogged-up glass, then dropped her towel.

Her heart pounded hard beneath her breast. She lifted her hand to it and traced the puckered flesh of the scar. While it was on her body, the scar was not hers. She'd had no injury that had inflicted it. She'd been born with it. Alaina had brought the scar with her from a former life. A life, and a death, she remembered only in flashes.

She hadn't seen enough yet to identify her killer. But somehow she knew that he was still out there—waiting to kill her. Again.

# Chapter 1

"Do you want me to call your lawyer?"

Trent Baines spun his chair away from the window that looked out over the thickly wooded hillside, the trees the fresh green of new life, of spring. His hands shaking slightly, he planted his palms on the shiny mahogany surface of his desk and said, "That's not necessary. I don't need a lawyer to talk to her."

"But she's with the FBI," Dietrich said, the big man's deep voice pitched low as if he worried she would overhear him, although he stood close to Trent's desk and she was on the other side of the doors, at least. Probably down the hall in the living room or foyer. Dietrich was paid well to protect Trent's privacy.

A grin tugged at Trent's mouth. "Do you think I've done something that puts me in need of a lawyer?"

"I didn't mean to imply…"

"Do you think the FBI has a valid reason for questioning me?"

"Sir—"

Trent lifted a hand to wave off his employee's contrition. "I'm just messing with you, Dietrich."

Anything to get a reaction out of the usually expressionless man—and to distract himself from what awaited him outside the pocket doors of his mahogany-paneled den. Fate.

He drew in a deep, bracing breath and directed his assistant. "Show her in."

"She's not alone," the other man reminded him.

Trent shrugged. "I don't care who's with her. I'll only see her."

He had already *felt* her, drawing nearer as she drove up to the estate. Even if he hadn't had the call to warn him, he would have known she was coming. With a connection this strong, she had to be the one.

He had to be the one. Everything had led her here—to him. Trent Baines had to be the killer.

"He will see you."

Startled, Alaina whirled away from the window and its fog-enshrouded view of the treetops. How had such a big man moved so quietly back into the living room where he'd left her and Agent Vonner? Then the young man, wearing a suit as dark as Vonner's, turned to leave again.

Vonner trailed after him and, her pulse racing, she followed Vonner. Their footsteps on dark slate flooring echoed in the two-story foyer through which they passed. On one side of it were the double doors from which they'd entered. On the other, an elaborate double staircase with a cathedral-size stained-glass window on the landing.

As Vonner had commented, the place was a castle. And only one man lived here, with his servants?

The butler or bodyguard—or whatever the

young man was—held out a hand as if stopping traffic at the closed pocket doors at the end of the wide hall. "Mr. Baines will only see the woman."

"Agent Paulsen," Alaina supplied her name.

"No," Vonner protested.

"It's fine," she said. Her gun heavy on the holster on her belt, she wasn't afraid for her safety.

The man—Dietrich he had called himself when he'd let them in earlier—began to slide open the pocket doors.

"You can't see him alone," Vonner protested and reached out to grasp Alaina's arm.

She glanced from the fingers crushing the sleeve of her dark suit jacket to his face. Then she arched a brow, uncertain of Vonner's motives. Did he not want her to get all the glory if they had, at last, found a genuine lead? Or was his concern only for her safety?

Neither option comforted her. In fact, she had been uneasy ever since Vonner had been assigned to the cold case with her. The male agent acted more interested in her than the case.

Vonner released her, but his dark-eyed gaze

had gone beyond her to the man standing inside the dark-paneled den. "He's not old enough…"

To be the killer? Was that what Vonner was about to say?

Alaina stepped away from her partner. As she joined Trent Baines in his inner sanctum, the pocket doors slid shut, closing her inside, alone with him. Despite what her partner believed, she knew Trent Baines could still be the killer. The cold cases they investigated now had occurred before *this* lifetime of his. Alaina was aware of *her* other life. Was he?

His gaze met hers, his green eyes burning with an intensity that had heat streaking through her body. Even though several feet separated them, she could feel not just the touch of his stare but the touch of his hands, caressing the curve of her waist, the slope of her hip, cupping the weight of her breasts.…

She could feel his skin sliding over hers as she lay naked beneath him, her hands clutching at the rippling muscles of his back. Images flashed through her mind, images of his face as he lowered his head to hers, his mouth touching her lips. But this man didn't look like Trent Baines, who had dark blond hair and penetrating green eyes. The man in the images had brown hair and eyes, but something about him was eerily similar to Trent, almost as if they were the same man.

Her lips parted, and a shaky breath escaped her aching lungs. Was he the man she had loved or the man who had killed her for loving someone else?

"You feel it, too," Baines remarked, his voice thick with a sexy huskiness.

"Feel what?" Her heart pounded with fear and emotion.

"The connection."

Determined to pull herself together, Alaina lifted her chin and arched a brow. "Not a very original come-on. I expected more creativity from a *New York Times* bestselling author."

"Are you a fan, Agent…?"

"Paulsen."

"Do you have a first name?"

"Yes."

His mouth, his lips full and unsettlingly sexy, curved into a grin. "You're not willing to share?"

"I don't think it's necessary for us to be on a

first-name basis, Mr. Baines," she said. Not when she could already feel his touch, his kiss… "I'm only here to ask you some questions."

"You don't want my autograph?" he asked, a teasing glint brightening his eyes. He reached behind him, onto his desk, and lifted a hardcover book. "I'd be happy to sign a copy for you. To your first name."

"I don't want a signed book." Or for him to know her first name. She already felt too intimately connected to him, more intimately connected than she'd felt to any other man she'd met…in this life. "I've read everything you've written."

Baines picked up a pen from the leather blotter on his desk and, as if he hadn't heard her, flipped through the first couple pages of the book. "So you are a fan."

"I'm an investigator."

He scribbled something and held out the book to her. She hesitated to step closer, but she couldn't reach it unless she moved nearer to where he sat now on the edge of his desk. He was tall, like his employee, but his body had the lean, muscular build of a runner. He obviously didn't spend all his time behind his desk. Yet how had he written so many books, and achieved so much success, at an age she guessed to be close to her own thirty years?

Curiosity overcame her reluctance, and she closed the distance between them. When she grasped the book, he pulled it back, tugging her nearer so that her thighs rubbed against his as she stumbled between his knees. Her heart slammed against her ribs as it began to beat furiously. "Mr. Baines—"

"Trent," he corrected her, his voice a raspy drawl. "Call me Trent."

She shook her head, hoping to break the hold he had on her—the one that was more emotional than physical. "I didn't come here for your autograph. I'm not a fan, Mr. Baines."

His shoulders rippled beneath his thin black T-shirt as he shrugged. "I have few fans in law enforcement."

"I'm surprised you have any," she remarked.

He released the book she hadn't realized she still held, and advised, "Read the autograph."

Her fingers trembling slightly, she opened the cover and flipped to the title page, to the masculine scrawl of his signature and the words above it. *To Alaina, I feel it, too.*

She lifted her gaze from the book to his face. With sculpted features and those sexy lips, the man was beyond handsome. He was fascinating. "You know my name."

His grin flashed again. "I'm an investigator, too."

"Your editor called you," she surmised because she had only been able to track him down through his publisher. The man had gone to extremes to protect his privacy.

"Of course. The publisher makes too much money off me not to take care of me," he said with glib arrogance. But his green eyes sparkled with amusement, as if he laughed at himself.

"And Dietrich?" she asked, referring to the man who'd shown her to his den. "Does he take care of you, too? Is he your butler or your bodyguard?"

"He's my assistant."

"So you don't do your own research?" she asked, wondering now if she was talking to the wrong man. But then he moved, and his knee rubbed against the side of her thigh. Her pulse raced in reaction and she knew…this was the man. She stepped back, needing some distance between them, needing to not touch him.

"I'm not sure what exactly Dietrich assists me with," he said, his brow furrowing in confusion, "but it's not my writing. No one helps me with that."

Her hand shaking slightly, she closed the hardcover book. "So you've done all your own research for this series?"

He nodded. "Do you want some investigative pointers?"

A smile threatened, but she bit her bottom lip. She should have been irritated instead of amused by his arrogance. "I am here because I want some information."

"What do you want to know, Alaina?"

Her name on his lips lifted goose bumps along her skin and the fine hairs on the nape of her neck. "I want to know how you found out details that were never released to the public."

He arched a dark blond brow. "Details of what?"

"Of the murders you sensationalized in your books."

"Sensationalized?" He tapped a finger against the spine of the book she held. "It's fiction."

Her stomach muscles tightened in dread. "No, it's not. Every one of those murders actually happened."

And one of those murders had been hers.

## Chapter 2

"No, no, they haven't." Trent denied the veracity of her claim even though he knew she spoke the truth. For some time he had suspected that the images in his head weren't products of an overactive imagination but memories. Someone else's memories. "It's fiction," he insisted. "Just fiction."

"I have case files—"

"I want to see them," he demanded.

He hadn't wanted to know before, so he had never looked up old news stories or pulled police records. But now he needed proof; he needed to prove that the murders in his books didn't match the ones about which Agent Paulsen had come to question him.

She shook her head with enough force that one silky tendril of blond hair slipped free of the knot at the back of her head. "That isn't possible."

"Why not?" he challenged her. "Are you afraid I'd write about them? According to you, I already have."

"Yes, it's like those poor women have been brutally murdered twice," she said. "Once in reality and then again in your novels."

Trent squeezed his eyes shut on a wave of self-disgust. "I didn't know."

Because he hadn't let himself believe…

"You had to know. You used too many details," she said, releasing a shaky sigh. "You used *every* detail, some that had never been released, details of which very few people were aware."

"That's why you're here," he surmised.

"Of course. What other reason would I have?"

Because she'd been looking for him, as he'd been looking for her—for the woman with whom he knew he would share this special connection.

Yet even as connected as he was with her, he couldn't feel her emotions like he was able to experience the emotions of others. He had no idea if she was really feeling what he was. The fierce, breath-stealing attraction and heart-pounding desire.

"The police like to hassle me from time to time," he admitted. "I'm used to it."

"In your books the serial killer," she said, her pretty mouth twisting in disgust, "is the hero."

"I wouldn't call him a hero." Complex. Multi-dimensional. That was what the critics called the protagonist of Trent Baines's *Thief of Hearts* horror series.

"But," she said, "you've written him as being smarter than law enforcement."

That was what tended to piss off the authorities.

Her smoky gray-blue eyes darkened with frustration, and she added, "He always gets away."

"Didn't your killer?"

"What?" The faint color drained from her porcelain skin. "How do you know?"

"This killer you're after," Trent said even as he wondered at her reaction, wishing again that he could feel her emotions. "You wouldn't still be after him if he hadn't gotten away."

"How do you know I'm after him?"

"You wouldn't be here if you weren't. We've already established that you're not a fan." And she wasn't likely to become one now. Despite whatever they might have meant to each other in another time, he was the writer that law enforcement hated.

"I could just be following up on a case," she pointed out. "Checking out why you know things that only the killer would."

He swallowed hard, but the knot in his throat wouldn't go down. "*Only* the killer?"

Color rushed back into her face. "Or his victims."

"But none of his victims could have survived to share their stories," Trent said. If those real murders were exactly like the ones in his books, in his mind, no one could have survived the brutal attacks, the ritualistic mutilation. But they could have come back, returning from the dead into a new life.

Was that what had happened to him? Had he lived before? Was that why he had these memories that were not his? Whose were they, then? The memories of the killer that Alaina Paulsen sought?

"No, none of his victims survived," she confirmed.

"How long ago did the murders happen?"

"I didn't come here to share information with you," she reminded him.

"You came here to get information from me." The irony had his lips twitching into a grin. How could a man who had no idea what was real and what was fiction aid in a federal investigation?

"So tell me, Mr. Baines," she persisted, "how you know things no one else knows about these murders."

He tapped a fingertip against his forehead. "Imagination, Alaina." That was what he'd been telling himself the past ten years—that he was only imagining things.

But he wasn't imagining the connection between him and this woman, this stranger. Needing to touch her, he reached out, but before his fingertips could skim her cheek, she caught his wrist.

"Don't." She dropped his arm and stepped back, increasing the distance between them.

But he could still feel her touch, his skin tingling where her fingers had held his wrist.

"You might be able to ignore it, but I can't," he said. "There's something here...." Something in her that pulled at him, that drew him to her. "There's something between us."

"Your ego," she quipped.

He laughed. Sick of adoring fans, he found her attitude refreshing and attractive. But then, he found everything about her attractive. "Alaina..."

"These books," she said as she lifted the one she still held, "these murders, aren't from just your imagination. They are exactly the same as the real ones."

He shrugged again. "Haven't you heard? There is no such thing as an original idea."

"I've heard that, but the saying I believe is that there is no such thing as coincidence." She narrowed her eyes. "There's no way you have all those details exactly the same by coincidence."

"I don't believe in coincidence, either," he admitted. "I believe in fate, Alaina. I think that's what brought you here." He stood and closed the distance between them. This time when he reached for her, she didn't catch his wrist. She didn't stop him. His fingertips slid along the curve of her cheekbone, then down her neck to where her pulse pounded fast and hard beneath her pale skin. "Fate is what brought you to me."

Her throat moved as she swallowed. Then her tongue slid out from between her lips, sliding over the fuller bottom one.

Trent leaned forward, drawn to her mouth, to her lips. But before he could taste more than her breath, the doors rattled under a pounding fist.

"Alaina, c'mon," a male voice called out to her. Trent felt and heard the man's impatience. "We have to go!"

As close as Trent was to her, just a breath apart, he caught the flash of regret in Alaina's eyes before she pulled back.

"No, you have to stay," Trent urged her.

She shook her head and, with a trembling hand, pulled a cell phone from her pocket. "I—I have to go."

"You will come back," he said.

"Yes," she said to his relief, but then she dashed his hopes. "But just because you haven't answered any of my questions."

He shook his head. "No, because you won't be able to stay away from me."

She didn't deny his claim. She just pulled open the doors and walked away, joining her impatient partner in the hall, so she didn't hear his next words.

"And because I won't be able to stay away from you…"

She turned back, their gazes meeting, holding like he'd longed to hold her. And he suspected that she knew, even if she hadn't heard him.

"What the hell was going on in there?" Vonner asked.

Fortunately, he had to concentrate on the hairpin turns of the tree-lined road leading away from Trent Baines's remote hilltop estate in the Upper Peninsula of Michigan. So he couldn't see Alaina's face, which was certain to reveal everything she felt: stunned, overwhelmed and disappointed. Leaving Trent Baines hadn't been easy; staying away would probably prove as hard as he'd warned her.

She stared at the facedown book on her lap. His publicity shot added to the mystery surrounding the reclusive author, as his raised hand covered most of his face. Only the strong line of his jaw and wind-tousled dark blond hair were visible around his palm and fingers.

"Alaina?" Vonner prodded her. "What happened in there? What was going on?"

Fighting to steady her voice, she said, "I don't know what you mean.…"

"Why'd you waste so much time?" the dark-haired agent persisted. "He's not the guy. According to Igor—"

"Igor?"

"His butler," Vonner explained. "According to him, Baines is only twenty-nine years old. As we both know, the last of these murders happened thirty years ago. Whatever Baines knows about the cases, he probably just figured out by reading old newspaper articles or talking to someone who was around back when the murders happened."

"But now there's been another murder." She reminded him of the call she hadn't heard because she'd been too distracted. Or captivated.

Trent Baines had nearly kissed her. And she

was disappointed that he hadn't, that they had been interrupted before she'd learned how his lips would feel, how his mouth would taste....

Guilt gripped her now. While she'd been distracted, someone else had been murdered. Brutally. Ritualistically. The M.O. exactly matched those thirty-year-old cases.

"This murder is further proof that Baines can't be the killer," Vonner added. "Because you were with him when we got the call."

"We don't know how long ago the murder occurred." Due to a weak cell signal, Alaina hadn't heard much of what her supervisor had said except that she needed to quit wasting her time on an unsubstantiated lead.

Only she knew it wasn't unsubstantiated. Only she knew that Baines had used details that weren't even in the files of those cold cases. But if she told her bosses how she knew—that she remembered a past life...and *death*—she'd lose whatever respect and credibility she had in the Bureau. They would think she was as crazy as the killer.

"The guy's so isolated up here," Vonner pointed out, cursing beneath his breath as a tire dropped off the edge of the drive onto the loose gravel shoulder. "There are no quick trips for him."

"We can't rule him out yet," she insisted, "not until we have more information about the murder."

"They're not going to release the scene until we get there," Vonner assured her. "But still I can't see how Baines is involved."

And Alaina couldn't see how he couldn't be involved. He knew too much—and made her feel too much—to not be deeply involved.

With the murders?

Or just her?

He'd found her. Or had she found him?

With her blond hair and grayish eyes, she didn't look or sound or smell the same, but then she was in a different body. Only her soul and her spirit had returned in the beautiful form of Alaina Paulsen.

This time she would love *him,* only him. And if, like last time, she refused to give him her heart, he'd just have to take it.

Again.

# Chapter 3

Emotion overwhelmed him. This was why he isolated himself in the wooded hills of his estate—because he couldn't block out what others were feeling. He couldn't help but feel it, too.

Disgust and fear emanated from the uniformed officers guarding the door. Trent passed them and ducked under the yellow tape. The crime scene had already been processed, so he was alone in the studio apartment. The victim's body was on its way to the morgue, but he could feel the residual emotion left in the room.

The paralyzing terror hung heavy in the air. He winced as the echo of the victim's screams reverberated inside his head. He widened his eyes as he studied the scene—the blood spattered on the white walls and drying to a dark burgundy, the blood pooled on the hardwood floor, as thick and dark as tar. He inhaled deeply, trying to fill his shallow lungs, but he breathed in the cloying metallic scent of blood.

His stomach cramped, and he doubled over, crippled with pain. But the pain was not his. It was never his. He always felt others' pain, others' emotions. Never his own.

Until today. Until he'd met Alaina Paulsen.

"What the hell!" a vaguely familiar male voice exclaimed in surprise.

"How— Why are you here?" asked a woman. *The* woman—Alaina Paulsen.

Like earlier today when he'd been with her, Trent felt none of her emotions. He felt no emotions but his own. Attraction, fascination and an overwhelming sense of destiny…

"You can't be here," the man said.

Trent assumed he was the other agent, the one he'd refused to see because he'd only been able to see her. This time he took a moment to compose himself, schooling his features back into his usual cocky mask, before he straightened up and turned to her.

"How did you get here before us?" Alaina asked.

"He must have a helicopter," her partner answered for Trent. The man stood close to her, protectively. Were they more than professional partners?

Trent didn't care what they'd been. The guy was no threat to him. No other man had the claim on her that he did. As he met her gaze, one emotion gripped him—possessiveness. *Mine*.

Her eyes widened, as if she'd read his mind, and she dragged in a shaky breath. "That explains how you got to Detroit before we did," she said, "but how did you get here?" She gestured at the apartment. "Into our crime scene."

The "our" to which she referred was not her and her partner; Trent couldn't accept that. It was him and her. She knew just as well as he did that he was part of this. If only he knew, for certain, which part.

"I told you," he reminded her. "I have a few fans in law enforcement."

"In the Bureau?" the male agent asked, his dark eyes narrowed with doubt. His suspicion was as palpable in the air as the scent of the victim's blood.

"Check out my story," Trent suggested, more to get rid of the guy than to reassure him.

The agent turned to Alaina, who offered a brief nod. With a warning glare at Trent, the man ducked under the crime-scene tape and slipped out into the hall.

"So you're the senior agent," Trent observed.

"What?"

"He checked with you before leaving." Or maybe her partner had just wanted to make sure she would be all right alone with Trent.

Alaina didn't satisfy his curiosity as she ignored his observation. "That's why I went to your estate," she said, "to check out your story. To find out what your involvement was in those old murders."

Her brow knitted as she glanced around the room, taking in the crime scene. Again, the color faded from her porcelain skin, leaving her ghostly pale.

But she wasn't a ghost. She was real. And for the first time in the memory of his own life, Trent felt real. His emotions were finally his own instead of what he'd empathetically picked up from someone or somewhere else.

"Those murders happened before I was born," he reminded her.

"You do have a friend in the Bureau," she said, accepting his claim without the confirmation her partner required. "A source."

He shrugged. "I wouldn't call him a source," he clarified. "More like a fan." Someone who had contacted him a couple times throughout the years and whom Trent had felt comfortable calling to find out all he could about Agent Paulsen—like where she'd rushed off to in such a hurry.

Before he'd had a chance to kiss her and test the strength of the passion she'd drawn from his soul…

"A fan?" She shook her head, as if she doubted his claim or doubted that anyone would actually enjoy the novels he'd written.

Sometimes he wondered about that himself. He didn't enjoy writing them; they exhausted him as much as experiencing the emotions of others.

"This murder didn't happen before you were born," she pointed out, her teeth nibbling at her full bottom lip. "Did you get sick of just writing about murder and decide to reenact one that you wrote about?"

"No." He wasn't a killer…in *this* life. But if he had the *soul* of a killer…

"No?" she repeated as if disappointed by his short response. "That's it? You're not going to eloquently profess your innocence?"

While he shrugged, he was anything but unconcerned. "It doesn't matter how eloquent I am. You've already made up your mind about me, Alaina."

"You're involved," she insisted. "Somehow, someway, you're involved."

He wished like hell that he wasn't. But he couldn't deny her allegations.

As if she dismissed him, she began to inspect the crime scene, ignoring his presence.

He couldn't ignore her; he could do nothing but stare at her.

Then she uttered a sudden gasp.

He followed her gaze to discover what had elicited the reaction from her. The blood, the gore? He would have expected that she was used to those things in crime scenes. Then he saw it, too: his book, lying atop the daybed where the victim had been raped and mutilated. The book lay facedown, the hand lifted over Trent's face in the publicity shot spattered with blood.

As if he hadn't already been blaming himself for this woman's death…

Her blood was on his hand. It had only been a book, Alaina kept reminding herself. But still she couldn't get the image out of her head. She couldn't get Trent out, either. She worried that he was in deeper than her mind, that he owned a part of her reincarnated soul.

"Why are you so hung up on Baines?"

She jerked away from her intense scrutiny of the bright lights of the cityscape outside her office window. Vonner's startling question brought forth a rage of denial and resentment. "Why the hell would you say something so—"

He held up a palm to interrupt her tirade and clarified, "As the killer. Why are you so hung up on him being the killer? Yeah, I get that the helicopter access makes him a suspect in this case, but he wasn't even alive when the other murders occurred."

She turned back to the window, leaving Vonner sitting in front of her desk piled high with cold-case files. She only needed to glance at one of the folders to know exactly what was inside; she'd read them all so many times. But how did Trent know so many of the details it had taken her years to learn? "He knows too much."

"So you think he knows who the killer is?" Vonner asked with a heavy sigh. "That he interviewed him when he started writing those horror books of his?"

He should have been excited by the lead he'd been chasing for months—Alaina for years—but they'd spent hours on the road after very little sleep. She understood his weariness.

But Alaina doubted she would sleep anytime soon. The killing had started again. She knew this murder would not be a onetime thing; she knew it with as much certainty as she knew the contents of every one of those cold-case files. This new victim's case would never get onto that pile on her desk; Alaina would not rest until Penelope Otten's murderer was found.

"Yes, I think he knows who the killer is." Or he had been the killer in another life and his evil soul had called him to kill again…?

She sucked in a breath at the horrific thought. She didn't want him to be the killer. She just wanted—

Vonner said, "We'll have to talk to him again."

That was what she was afraid of—talking to him, touching him, kissing him, giving in to the passion that had burned so hotly between them that it was forever a part of her soul. But she would do whatever was necessary to find the killer. "Yes, we'll need to interview him."

"That's if the bosses will let us." Vonner pushed a hand through his disheveled hair. "I still can't believe he was granted access to a crime scene."

"A crime he could have committed," she reminded her partner and herself. He could be a killer in this life, too.

"Think the Bureau will let us use the helicopter to get back to the U.P.?" he asked. "I hate to think of doing that drive again."

"He's here now," she murmured, her skin tingling as she sensed him close.

"What?"

"He's somewhere in the building," she said.

"What? Did Security notify you when he came in?" Vonner asked.

"Something like that…" Her phone rang, saving her from offering a more specific explanation. Her partner would not understand her special connection with the horror author; she didn't understand it herself.

Vonner grabbed the receiver. "Agent Paulsen's desk."

She held out her hand for the phone, but instead of passing it to her, he hung it up. "Who was that?" she asked.

"The morgue."

Trent gripped the edge of the metal table on which the victim's body lay. His vision blurred, a red haze blinding him as pain overwhelmed him. He felt every emotion she had experienced in those final moments before her death. Panic shortened his breath and quickened his pulse. Then the fear intensified to a terror so acute that his lungs burned with a scream he couldn't utter. His throat ached as if strong hands wrapped tight around his neck, choking the life from his body. But before the threatening blackness claimed him, the pressure eased. He gasped for breath, trying to fill his aching lungs. Then pain shot through his heart, so sharp and intense he clutched a hand to his chest and dropped to his knees.

"What's he doing?" a male voice whispered. "Having a heart attack?"

Trent turned toward where Alaina stood in the doorway to Autopsy. He hadn't felt her this time. He'd been too connected to the dead woman, to the emotions echoing from her soul within the empty shell of her mutilated body.

Those emotions clung to him no matter that he tried to shake them off. Exhaustion weighing heavy on his limbs, he lurched to his feet and staggered into the metal table. The woman's stiff arm dropped off the edge, her hand open as if reaching out to him.

Alaina stared at him, her eyes narrowed and

her brow slightly creased beneath the fall of blond hair. The man, her partner, stood almost in front of her, as if protecting her from Trent or trying to come between them.

A memory tugged at him, a memory of frustration and jealousy. Someone else had tried to come between them. In another life?

"What the hell's wrong with you?" Agent Vonner asked. "Are you drunk?"

He ignored the man as if he was invisible. To Trent he was; he could see only her now.

"What are you doing?" she asked him finally.

"I was given access—"

"To the Bureau's morgue?" Vonner asked, his voice cracking with shock and indignation. "Who the hell gave you access?"

Because she lifted a dark blond brow in question, Trent answered, "Phillip Graves."

A breath hissed out between Vonner's clenched teeth at the mention of the director's name. He turned his back on Trent and spoke softly to her. "We gotta stop this, Alaina. We can't have a suspect getting access to the crime scene and the evidence. We have to talk to the director."

"You need to talk to Agent Bilski first," she corrected her coworker as she slipped past him to stand on the opposite side of the metal table from Trent. "Don't go over his head."

"Okay, Bilski first," Vonner agreed. "But you have to come with me to talk to him."

She shook her head in denial.

Trent's lips twitched into an amused grin. She didn't like being told what to do. He could identify; he'd never liked taking orders.

"I can't leave you alone with *him*," Vonner said.

She lifted her gaze from the victim to Trent. "Where's Dr. Rosenthal?"

"He stepped out to get something for me," Trent admitted.

"What the hell? Are you ordering him around like you do that ape you have on your payroll?" Vonner asked.

"Oh, I'm glad you're still here," Dr. Rosenthal said as he rushed back into the room. "Thank you for waiting for me."

The gray-haired coroner's admiration and awe physically washed over Trent, drawing a smile from him even as Vonner's disgust and distrust pummeled him from the other side of the room. But he experienced none of Alaina's emotions. He could only *feel* her, like a touch on his skin, a kiss on his lips.…

Dr. Rosenthal held out a book and a pen to Trent. "Do you mind signing my copy for me?"

Trent steadied his hand as he reached for the book, the same edition that had been spattered with blood at the crime scene. Even though this cover was clean, he could see the blood again on his hand.

How was he involved in all of this? It was more than mere coincidence. He knew this. And so did she.

Vonner snorted and turned on his heel, leaving the room. Trent noted his exit, but Alaina didn't so much as glance at her partner. Instead, she stared at him, as if trying to figure out who he was or where she'd seen him before.

An image chased through Trent's mind. The curve of a woman's throat as she arched her neck. Her hands, with slender, red-tipped fingers, cupping and caressing her own breasts as she moved her hips, rocking back and forth on his pulsing erection. Then her cry of pleasure as she came. The woman had red hair and green eyes; she looked nothing like Alaina. But to him, she felt the same.

"Mr. Baines," the coroner said, glancing from him to Agent Paulsen. Confusion wrinkled his brow. "Do you mind autographing…?"

"Not at all," Trent assured him, flipping through until he came to the title page. Then he scrawled the doctor's name, some platitude and his own, although sometimes he didn't feel as if his name was really his. Even though he hadn't taken a pen name, Trent Baines felt like an alias; he felt as if he was really someone else.

"So, Dr. Rosenthal," Alaina said, drawing the coroner's attention away from him, "when will you have the autopsy report ready?"

"I need more time," Dr. Rosenthal said, his face flushing with color.

"How long?" Alaina asked sharply, her impatience with the doctor's lack of professionalism obvious.

"I can't tell you how long it will take me," the doctor said. "It's getting late.…"

"How long has she been dead?" she clarified.

"I did a liver temp. Twenty-four hours."

She glanced at Trent. No doubt he was back on her suspect list. Then she turned to the doctor again and advised, "Let me know as soon as you finish the autopsy. And don't call me again if you don't have any information for me."

Dr. Rosenthal sputtered, "B-but I didn't—"

"I called you," Trent admitted, irritation gripping him that the male agent had answered her phone.

"Why?" she asked.

"Because I can tell you what happened to her."

She said nothing, only turned that unfathomable stare on him again.

He continued, anyway. "She was raped, then strangled until she nearly blacked out."

Dr. Rosenthal gestured toward the victim's throat. "There is bruising around her neck that supports that."

"And then she was stabbed," he said with a twinge in his chest as he relived the woman's pain. He drew in a ragged breath before finishing his assessment, "And her heart removed from her chest."

The doctor did not need to point out the gaping hole and missing organ in the mutilated corpse. Dr. Rosenthal only added, "His M.O. is just like that of the protagonist in your books, just like the Thief of Hearts."

"Exactly like the Thief of Hearts," Alaina agreed, her eyes unblinking as she studied Trent.

Did she expect a confession?

## Chapter 4

"I want to talk to you," Alaina said from the shadows of the dimly lit corridor. She'd waited for Trent outside the morgue, unwilling to watch the coroner continue to fawn over the author. And she'd been unable to stand beside the body of the red-haired woman who'd died such a violent death—the same death Alaina was certain she had experienced.

Trent grinned as if not a bit surprised to find her in the hall, waiting for him. Then he reminded her, "I warned you that you wouldn't be able to stay away from me."

Heat flushed her skin as she remembered what he'd told her when she'd left him that morning. Then another memory flashed through her mind: a thumb stroking across her bottom lip, back and forth. A hungry mouth sliding down her throat, nibbling along her collarbone before skimming over the slope of her breast to the nipple that peaked, begging for attention. His attention.

She swallowed hard, choking down the desire that overwhelmed her. "I only want to talk to you."

His naughty, sexy grin widened as he stepped closer to her, trapping her against the wall. "Why waste our time talking?" he asked, his voice a seductive purr. "I'm not going to tell you what you want to hear."

"What's that?" She leaned her head back, away from the temptation of his lips. "What do I want to hear?"

"That I'm the killer."

"If only it were that easy…" She sighed, bone-deep weary from a day that had started with her and Vonner on the road at dawn, driving up to Trent Baines's remote castle in the Upper Peninsula. Now, night had fallen and she was back where she'd started in Detroit…only with Trent Baines. Just as he'd said, she couldn't stay away from him.

The image flashed through her mind again— lips tugging at her nipple, a tongue flicking across the tip, hands caressing her back, then along her sides to the curve of her hips. She arched and parted her legs, silently begging for him to take her.…

But he pulled back.

Trent stepped away from her and asked, "Killers don't spontaneously confess like on television?" His green eyes sparkled with feigned innocence.

"No one who'd actually committed a crime ever spontaneously confessed to me." She crossed her arms across her chest. It was cold in the hall, but her skin was hot, flushed with desire for the man in her mind.

And maybe the one in the hall…

"Innocent people confess?" he asked.

"Innocent? I don't know how innocent they are when they interfere with an investigation just to get attention. Screwed up, yeah." But then, so was she, to be attracted to a man who might be a killer.

He lifted his shoulders in a slight shrug. "Well, I'm not going to confess either my guilt or innocence. You're wasting your time talking to me."

"And you're wasting your time going to the crime scene, visiting the morgue." Tension pounded at her temples and knotted the muscles in her neck and shoulders. "What are you doing here in the middle of my investigation?"

"I got clearance."

"But why would you ask for it? Why would you want to go to a crime scene or visit the morgue?" She had to know. "Is this what you do? Is this how you research your novels?"

"That's what the director thinks," he admitted with a wink. "But I'm really not one to do much research."

"Then I'll ask you again. What are you doing here?" Trying to cover up evidence that might have implicated him? Sure, the crime scene had already been processed, the evidence collected, before he'd arrived. But still his presence there, and at the morgue, unsettled her, raising her suspicions about him even more.

He stepped forward again and touched her, just the pad of his thumb sliding along the line of her jaw. "I'm here for you."

She shivered at the intensity of his gaze and the heat of his touch. Both felt eerily familiar. "Why? You won't answer my questions."

"I want to help you, Alaina," he said, his deep voice full of seductive promise. "I want you to figure out what you need to know."

"I need to know who this killer is," she said. "I need to catch him." She'd wanted that for so long, even before he'd killed again. Now she had to find him, to stop him....

"That's not all you need to know." He leaned closer, his forehead nearly touching hers. "You need to know about us."

She pushed her hands against his chest and shoved him back. Ignoring the tingling in her palms from the heat of his body and the hardness of his muscles, she shook her head. "There is no us. And there will never be."

But had there been? In another life? Was he the lover she dreamed of, even wide-awake? Was he the man who had loved her so passionately in her past life that no other man in this life had ever measured up?

"You feel it, Alaina," he insisted, his voice a rough whisper. "I know you feel it, too."

Staring into his eyes, she could almost glimpse the images in their depths, the images that had been taunting her, of two naked bodies intimately connected, physically and emotionally. Alaina dragged in a ragged breath of air and shook her head again, trying to clear it. "All I feel for you is suspicion. You know more than you're telling me about those old murders and this one."

His grin flashed again. "You feel more than that. You feel what I feel...."

It didn't matter what she felt. "I don't trust you," she stated unequivocally, reminding herself. "All I want is the truth."

"Since you don't trust me, you won't believe that anything I tell you is the truth," he pointed out. "So I guess we have nothing to talk about."

Images, like slides in a projector, flicked through her mind—a sculpted chest pressed against her breasts, heavily muscled arms holding her close, perspiration glistening on slick skin....

She opened, then closed, her mouth, knowing it was useless to ask Trent Baines any more questions. Like he'd said, she wouldn't trust the veracity of his answers.

But since she didn't trust anyone with her secrets, she couldn't expect him to share his willingly. She'd have to find out what she wanted to know another way.

"Come with me," he urged her, his green eyes glittering with desire and erotic promises. "Come with me and we won't have to talk at all."

Temptation pulled at her to see if he could deliver on those promises. To see if he could make her feel what she only imagined....

*"I shouldn't be here," she whispered, as if afraid someone might overhear her and catch them. "It's so wrong...."*

*"That's what makes it so exciting," he pointed out as he reached for her.*

*She pressed her palms against his chest, as if about to push him away again. Her eyes wide with confusion, she stared up at him. "I don't know why I'm here."*

*"I told you," he reminded her, "that you wouldn't be able to stay away from me…any more than I can stay away from you. You belong with me."*

*She shook her head, trying to deny him, trying to deny her feelings.*

*He cupped her chin in his hand and tipped her face up. "Look at me. I'm the man you're meant to be with. You can feel it, too." He lowered his lips and just brushed them across hers. "When I kiss you…" He trailed his fingers across her cheek, along the length of her neck to the curve of her breast. "When I touch you…"*

*Her fingers clenched the fabric of his shirt, dragging him closer. "I want you."*

*Want. It wasn't love. And what he wanted—needed—was her love.*

The soft click of a door opening drew Trent's attention from his computer screen. He lifted his head as Dietrich stepped inside his room of the hotel suite they shared.

"I'm sorry, sir," the big man said. "I didn't mean to interrupt your writing."

"No, that's fine." He didn't want to be writing, anyway; he wanted to be with Alaina. But she had refused his proposition and denied her feelings for him.

Hell, maybe he was wrong about her. Maybe he couldn't feel what she felt because she felt nothing for him. Maybe this connection between them, this sense of destiny, was only in his mind.

Trent rubbed a hand across his forehead where tension pounded with the onslaught of the emotions of others. "Did you get this floor cleared?"

Dietrich nodded. "The concierge helped convince them to move to the new rooms you're paying for."

"And everyone moved?" Because he could still feel the anxiety of someone about to do something… Apply for a new job? Ask someone to marry him?

And the couple that fought…

Trent felt their anger and resentment, the hurt and pain that felt eerily familiar even though he'd never been in a relationship that had lasted beyond a week or two of physical pleasure.

At least, he hadn't in this life.

Had he lived before? Or was it that through

their emotions he lived everyone else's life right now?

Dietrich nodded. "Everyone on this floor has moved. But there are people on the floor below and in the buildings surrounding this hotel. We should go home, where it's quiet and peaceful," he urged. "The city is too much for you."

Trent closed his eyes as a red haze of emotion rushed over him. Then oblivion, black and comforting, tempted him to slip into unconsciousness. He'd done it before. Blacked out when he was too overwhelmed to deal with the pain of others.

At the crime scene and the morgue, he'd nearly lost consciousness. The terror and pain had been so intense.

But he was stronger now than the kid he'd once been…the kid who'd escaped into his own little world so he wouldn't have to deal with others. He opened his eyes to the screen of his laptop. The words he'd just written all blurred together unintelligibly.

And he realized it hadn't been his own little world.

Other people had lived in it with him… Before *he* had killed them?

Dietrich cleared his throat, drawing Trent's attention back to where he hovered, like a mother hen, in the doorway of the suite. He spoke hesitantly, dropping each word softly into the silence. "I don't understand why we're here."

Trent leaned back in his chair at the desk. Too weary to speak, he just arched a brow.

"You have that book to finish."

He'd already missed his deadline.

"Your editor called again today." Dietrich relayed the message, as much secretary as bodyguard. "Twice."

Evan was pissed, not just about the deadline but because Trent had told him this book would be the last in the lucrative *Thief of Hearts* series. It was time to end it. But he'd been struggling before Alaina Paulsen had shattered his peace and quiet and confirmed that his fiction was actually fact.

Fact that Trent didn't know if he was strong enough yet to face.…

"I'll get the book done," he promised Dietrich and himself.

"But it's easier for you to write back at the estate," his assistant insisted. "You have fewer distractions."

It wasn't just his empathy that distracted him now; it was her. And Dietrich must have noticed.

Hell, Trent had left shortly after she had that morning. But it hadn't been just that he was drawn to her, connected in some way he couldn't explain. It had been because of the murder. He'd called the Bureau to find out why she'd been called away so abruptly and he'd learned of it. The ritualistic killing that so closely matched the M.O. of the protagonist of his *Thief of Hearts* novels. He'd had to see for himself if the nightmares he'd hoped were only products of his imagination matched the horrifying reality.

"I was there," he murmured, the dead woman's terror gripping him again. "It was just like…" The violent images once again took center stage in his mind.

"It's not your fault," Dietrich said, "if someone copied your book. You can't be held responsible for someone else's actions."

But what if they'd once been his?

He closed his eyes, and passionate images replaced the violent ones. A woman's nails raking his back, clutching at his butt as he thrust inside her again and again. Alaina Paulsen was more than just an agent investigating murders; she was part of it, too.

She had once been his…and he couldn't leave until she was again.

Excitement coursed through him, but he fought it down, fought to control his emotions.

But it was all so perfect…

He wanted to scream, wanted to thump his fist in the air in celebration. But he had rejoiced another way, a far more satisfying way.…

He lifted the cover from the box. He'd found it, like he had so many other things, when he'd opened that door and allowed the past to come rushing back into his mind.

A chuckle rumbled in his chest. Trent Baines had unlocked that door with his books. And until today the man had had no idea that he'd let the monster loose.

He gazed inside that box at the heart he'd stolen. In his mind, it beat yet. For him…

But it wasn't the heart he really wanted. That

heart beat now inside Alaina Paulsen's chest. But he knew to whom it had once belonged. The woman she had once been and the man she had once loved…

Now he knew who they all were and who they all had once been…before he'd killed them.

He closed the lid on the box, which would soon fill with more hearts. Because now he knew what he had to do, who he had to kill. Again.

## Chapter 5

"So did you talk to the director?" Alaina asked as Vonner dropped into the chair across from her desk. Dust danced in the morning sun streaming through the windows. Since she'd forbidden the night-shift cleaners from touching her office, and potentially misplacing some of those files, she'd have to clean it herself soon.

After taking a swig of coffee from his paper cup, Vonner grimaced and shook his head. "No. I talked to Bilski first, like you suggested."

"And?"

He shrugged. "He doesn't think Baines is a problem."

Alaina rubbed her fingers over her tired eyes. She hadn't slept at all last night, plagued by the images chasing through her mind. Of that poor woman…and Trent, leaning close to her in the hall, his eyes promising her the passion she remembered from another life. Maybe she should have gone with him, wherever he'd wanted to take her. Maybe she should have let him take her.…

Maybe then she would have had the answers she'd sought for so many years.

She opened her eyes and focused on the pile of cold cases. Which woman had she been of the twelve murdered at the hands of a sadistic serial killer?

"You and I both know better," Vonner prodded her.

"What?" Heat flushed her face. She did know better than to trust a man who could have been that killer.

"We both know that Baines is a problem," Vonner explained. "A big one."

Yes, a problem for her peace of mind. For her heart…

But was he the killer? God, she hoped not.

"So Bilski wouldn't speak to the director?" she asked, trying to follow the conversation when she was tempted instead to follow her heart.

"No." Vonner snorted his disgust. "He figures Baines already left."

A twinge of regret tightened her chest. She rubbed her knuckles over it, feeling the faint ridge of the scar beneath the thin fabric of her lightweight sweater. She closed her eyes again, as an image taunted her.

Lips on her breast, the skin smooth and clear over her heart. Hands tightening on her hips, lifting her to meet his thrusts…

She opened her eyes, trying to clear her head, and she met his deep green gaze. Trent Baines stood behind Vonner, leaning against the open door of her small office. Heat rushed to her face as if he'd caught her like she'd been in that memory—naked and vulnerable.

"Good morning," he greeted them.

Startled, Vonner jerked and inadvertently squeezed his paper cup. Coffee surged between the rim and the lid and ran over his fingers. He set the cup on the floor and cursed.

Trent clicked his tongue against his teeth. "I figured you'd have sharper reflexes, being an agent."

"Damn you."

He shook his head. "You better run some cold water over that. Looks like it could be a nasty burn."

Vonner, his dark eyes hot with anger, glanced back at Alaina. "Go ahead," she assured him. "I can show Mr. Baines out."

"Show me out?" he asked after Vonner knocked against him, passing him in the doorway.

She rose from behind her desk and walked around it, blocking it and those files from his view. This was her personal space; she wanted him nowhere near it. "You must be leaving, right? Heading back to the U.P.?"

"Not yet," he said, his gaze intent on her face, as if he knew what she'd been thinking, what she'd been seeing.

"There's no reason for you to stick around," she pointed out. "You won't talk."

"There's another reason for me to stick around," he said, leaning close.

She needed to step back, to get away from him, in case he tried to kiss her. Because somehow she knew that if his lips touched hers, she'd be lost.

But instead of kissing her, he murmured, "I need to see those cold-case files."

She stepped closer to him, tempted to shove him out the door. "You exploited those women enough already," she said, anger choking her. "You're not using them anymore."

"I only have your word that my books match those murders," he said.

"You were there yesterday, at the crime scene." It still galled her that he'd beaten her there. "You know those murders match the books."

"No, I know *that* murder matched my books." And it drove him crazy that that woman might have died because of him, because some lunatic had decided to copy what he'd written. Or what he'd done.

"It's the same as the others," she insisted. "There's no need for you to go through the files."

"You should want me to take a look at them," he said. "I can help you."

She shook her head, and while he couldn't feel her emotions, he glimpsed the fear in the depths of her gray-blue eyes. Maybe, like him, she was afraid of the answers to the questions, afraid of what she would learn about herself. "What makes you think I need your help?"

"You came to me," he reminded her.

"For answers. You haven't given me any." Her eyes narrowed with suspicion. "You have nothing to offer me."

His lips twitched, and he grinned at her challenge. "We both know I have a lot to offer you."

He had to touch her, so he reached out to skim his fingertips along her delicate jaw. But she pulled back so his skin just brushed hers. It was enough that he felt her heat. And he knew that if he ever really touched her, passion would burn between them, brighter and hotter than even those images that flashed through his mind. "I can give you pleasure...."

"You arrogant bastard," she said. "You might

be used to women falling at your feet. But I'm not a fan. You don't impress me."

"Has any man?" he wondered. Or had she spent her life as he had, searching for something, for someone, he hadn't been able to find? Until now.

"My personal life is none of your damn business," she told him.

"Do you have one?" he wondered. "The director told me you've been working this case for a long time, almost obsessively." He narrowed his eyes, studying her face, wishing he could feel what she felt. But only his own emotions—his attraction and fascination with her—consumed him. And others' emotions edged in: pain, frustration, anger and resentment. "Why does this case mean so much to you, Alaina?"

"Every case means a lot to me," she said, but her voice lacked the strength of conviction.

"This case is personal to you," he said. "Why? Was one of those women your mother? Sister? Aunt?" Or, as he suspected, her?

"No."

"C'mon, Alaina, let me help you," Trent urged her. "You've gone over those files so many times that I'm sure you've missed something. I can be your fresh eyes, your fresh perspective."

"She doesn't need you," a deep voice informed him. The surly agent had returned. The cold water must have soothed away the burn of the hot coffee, for his fingers weren't red anymore.

Yet Trent saw the red in his mind, as if he weren't the only one with blood on his hands. Maybe he was just projecting, looking for someone else to blame for what he'd caused.

Vonner stated, "I'm her fresh eyes on this case."

"You just recently got assigned to it?"

Vonner nodded. "Unless you're willing to tell us who fed you the information from those files, you really have no reason to be here." The guy's dark gaze flicked to Alaina, as if staking his claim. "Why don't you end your little field trip to the FBI and go back home, Baines?"

"I have every reason to be here." And she stood right in front of him, her eyes narrowed with distrust. She was smart not to trust him when he didn't even trust himself.

Vonner was right; Trent needed to leave. It was better if he returned to the oblivion in which he'd been living. No emotions, others' or his own. No desires, like the passion that burned inside him for her.

As he met her gaze, he saw another woman, one with red hair and pale skin, standing naked before him, her lips curved into a smile of pure temptation. Her image superimposed over Alaina's until the two became one, as if the soul of the red-haired woman lived inside Alaina's beautiful face and body.

It had to be her....

She shivered, despite the turtleneck she wore beneath her dark suit jacket. She'd worn a high-necked sweater yesterday, too. He'd understood it up north, where the wind was cold even this late in spring. But here, in the warmth of the city, he didn't understand her conservative dressing.

Was it so she would be taken seriously as a female agent? Or was it to protect herself, to hide away the sensual woman he was certain she'd once been? The one who'd made love to him so thoroughly he could still feel her touch, her fingertips sliding over him, her lips closing around him....

"Baines?" Vonner snapped his fingers, as if

trying to break the connection between Trent and Alaina.

He was certain someone else had tried the same thing…at another time. Resentment and anger surged through him, familiar and too powerful to be ignored.

Maybe he had been what he feared most—the monster about which he'd written his bestselling series. And maybe, if he stayed here, with her, where he felt more than he'd ever felt before, he would become that monster again.

"You're right," he told Vonner. "I need to leave…" Before he did something, and became someone, that they would all regret.

Alaina almost ignored the ringing of her cell, but with a resigned sigh, she pulled the phone out of her pocket. "Agent Paulsen."

"Where'd you go?" Vonner asked.

"Home," she said as she pulled into the apartment complex parking lot. As late as it was, only spaces far from the building were empty.

"I need you here," Vonner insisted, "to talk to the director with me."

She sighed, her frustration with her overzealous partner growing. "Bilski told you not to—"

"But he was wrong about Baines. The guy is a problem."

"The guy left," she reminded him. "He went back to the U.P."

Vonner uttered an expletive. "He lied to us. He didn't go anywhere. He just walked in with the director right now. They went to dinner together."

"The director's a fan of his books," she said, just as Baines had claimed. Maybe she could trust him....

"The director's a fool to let him get this close to the case," Vonner said, his disgust apparent. "Baines is one of those guys we learned about in profiling classes. The serial killers who try to help solve the murders they themselves committed."

"You were the one who pointed out he's too young, that he wasn't even alive when those old murders occurred," she reminded him. "There's no way he could have been the killer." Except there was one way...

"Maybe he's the apprentice to the original killer, who's too old and weak now to commit the murders himself," Vonner rationalized. "So

Baines has taken over and is doing his killing for him."

"Do you have any proof to support your suspicions?" she asked. Because she needed some. She needed something to remind herself that Trent Baines could be a dangerous man and not just a sexy, attractive one.

"No, but—"

"When you do, then we'll talk to the director," she promised.

"It may be too late by then," Vonner warned. "We have to do something about him *now,* Alaina."

"Go home," she advised her partner as she shut off her Chevy TrailBlazer.

Vonner had been out all day, interviewing Penelope Otten's family, friends, coworkers and neighbors, searching for some lead on the killer. She had stayed back at the office, going over the old files, trying to figure out how that killer from thirty years ago could have begun killing again.

She'd checked the rational ways. For recent parolees. For recently released psychiatric patients.

But she suspected there was no rational explanation for how the Thief of Hearts had begun killing again.

"Let me come over to your place, then," Vonner implored. "We need to talk about how we're going to handle Baines."

She didn't want to handle Baines, to touch him, to kiss him....

God, she wished he'd gone back to his secluded estate. She needed to get some distance from him, some perspective. Images kept flashing through her head, images of a naked man, caressing her skin, kissing her lips, her throat....

But that man wasn't Trent Baines. It couldn't be.

"Alaina," her partner prodded her. "Tell me how to get to your place."

"No." Vonner didn't know where she lived, and she intended to keep it that way. "It's late. Go home. We'll talk in the morning." She clicked off the cell and shoved it back into her pocket, then she stepped out of her vehicle, slamming the door closed behind her.

Tall pines blocked the light from the streetlamps and cast shadows across the asphalt. The hair on her nape prickled as a cold wind rushed over her. She was not alone. Someone was watching her.

She reached beneath her jacket and rested her hand on her holster, so that she would be ready. She would not be a victim. Again.

Of course she was probably overreacting. With the size of the complex, anyone could have been coming or going. People worked all different shifts. Or, unlike her, they had social lives. Went out to dinner, watched movies. Dated.

But with the sound of heavy footsteps behind her, she closed her fingers over the gun handle and whirled around to confront her potential stalker.

"Dietrich!" she exclaimed in surprise.

"Mr. Baines sent me to give you this," the man said, his voice calm and his eyes devoid of fear or even surprise despite staring down the barrel of her gun.

"How did you know where I live?" she asked, the hair still lifted on her nape, the fear clinging to her despite the fact, or because, she'd identified the threat.

And Dietrich, with his hulking size and strange

demeanor, was a threat. She kept the gun trained on him as she edged closer to the building and the security lighting.

He followed her and held out a box, on the top of which her address had been scribbled in familiar handwriting. "Mr. Baines gave me directions, too."

As if he'd already driven past her place himself. How had Trent Baines known exactly where she lived?

She shivered despite the warm breeze. But she refused to let him intimidate her. She did, however, study the box, trying to determine what the twelve-inch by twelve-inch by six-inch-deep box could hold. "What's inside?"

The man's monster-wide shoulders rose and fell in a heavy shrug. "I don't know."

She believed him, although with his lack of expression, it would be nearly impossible to tell if he lied. But the box was sealed, Baines's handwriting scrawled across some of the tape. Unless Dietrich had seen what his employer had put inside, he could have had no idea of the contents.

Thinking about what had been missing from

every crime scene—from every victim—including the most recent one, Alaina had an idea of what could be in the box. But she hoped like hell she was wrong…about everything.

# Chapter 6

*Her breath escaped through parted lips. As her eyes widened in surprise, her body stiffened. But he wouldn't let her stop moving. His hands grasped her hips, pulling her up and dragging her back down the hard length of his shaft.*

*A groan tore from his throat as she came, pouring hot sensation over him. He wouldn't let her finish so quickly, though. He reached between them, rubbing his thumb against her most sensitive spot. Then he arched his back, lifting up from the mattress, and skimmed his mouth across the slick skin of her breast. He closed his lips around the nipple, biting gently before stroking his tongue across the peak.*

*She screamed his name, her body shattering in his arms. Then, finally, he released his tenuous hold on control, bucking beneath her, slamming in and out of her wet heat until his world exploded with a powerful orgasm.*

*And love. He loved her.*

A pounding noise abruptly drew Alaina's attention from the pages of the galley of Trent Baines's yet-to-be-published novel. Her fingers trembled as she reluctantly dropped the copy onto her soft cotton sheets. She wanted to ignore the interruption…for so many reasons.

But the hammering persisted at her front door, echoing down the hall to her bedroom. She slipped from between the tangled sheets and reached for her robe. After belting it tightly around her waist, she left the room. But she couldn't leave behind the effect of Trent Baines's words. Heat flushed her skin, and her pulse raced, as if she'd been the woman in the book, the woman making love.

A sigh slipped through her lips, as she realized she couldn't remember the last time she had actually made love. She could remember neither the man nor the encounter.

Because no man had been *him*.

Was Trent Baines?

She knew who knocked, but still she opened the door…to Trent.

He leaned nonchalantly against the jamb, as if he hadn't been insistently pounding. As if he'd dropped by for a casual visit.

"You've been expecting me," he observed.

She nodded. "Ever since I received the galley you had delivered."

To her home. Had he been taunting her with the fact that he'd found out where she lived when he'd sent his assistant to personally deliver the copy of the book?

"I told you that I'm a good investigator, too," he reminded her as he flashed that arrogant, sexy grin. "I can help you with this case."

"And I told you that I didn't want your help."

As if she'd invited him inside, he stepped through the door and brushed past her, so close that his T-shirt-covered chest grazed her satin robe.

Her breath caught. "I only wanted you to

answer some questions. I can't answer any of yours."

He paced her living room, inspecting her Spartan furnishings more thoroughly than he'd checked out the crime scene. Because he'd been there before?

Despite what her superiors believed, she still considered Trent Baines a suspect in this most recent murder. And because she believed in reincarnation, she suspected him in the other murders, too. It wasn't the rational explanation her superiors would accept, though, so she had kept it to herself.

"No, I mean I can help you now," he said, momentarily turning his attention back on her. His green eyes glittered as his gaze traveled from her bare toes to her disheveled hair.

"So you're finally willing to answer questions?" She toyed with the lapel of her robe, lifting it against her neck to hide the top line of the faint white scar on her chest. "You can meet me at the office tomorrow, then, since you're still in town."

He shook his head. "I just left your office. That's what I mean, Alaina. I now have the clearance to help you, with the new case and the old ones."

She backtracked. He hadn't said he'd just left the director's office.

"You were in *my* office?" Without her there? She had few furnishings in her apartment because her office was where she really lived, where she spent all her time. This place was only where she slept, which was why, besides the bed, she had only a couch and a coffee table and two stools pulled to the kitchen counter.

"Yeah, I was in your office," he said, confirming her fear. "You had all the case files in there."

"You went through the files?" Just the files. What about her desk? Had he touched her things? The snow globes her mother sent her from each new city she visited? The picture of the two of them on the last vacation Alaina had taken? "Seriously, what do you have on the director?"

"He's a fan." He shrugged as if it didn't matter that he'd gone over not only her head but her boss's head, too. And he'd violated her space. Like he violated it now...

Done inspecting her apartment, he closed the

distance between them, backing her against the wall as he studied her face. "No makeup and you're still so damn beautiful."

She stiffened her backbone, refusing to react to either the fact that he'd caught her without makeup or that he'd complimented her despite it.

"You need to leave," she insisted. "Now."

As if he hadn't heard her at all, he ignored her command and reached out, tracing a fingertip along her jaw. "Have you read it yet?"

She closed her eyes, not wanting him to see her reaction to his touch or his written words, and admitted, "I started it…"

Like he was starting something, with his nearness, with his touch.

*He might be a killer.*

Vonner's rational explanation could be the right one—that Trent Baines might have learned the details of the old murders from the original Thief of Hearts before he began the killing himself.

She needed to use the defensive maneuvers she knew so well. With one knee and a finger, she could render him as helpless as he made her feel. Yet she couldn't quite bring herself to hurt him. Still, she needed to knock his hand away from her face and shove his body back from hers. But she couldn't bring herself to do that, either.

His hand moved, from her face to her throat. He traced a fingertip across the skin that quivered as her pulse pounded hard beneath it.

"I hope you're enjoying it," he murmured.

Confused, she opened her eyes, uncertain if he referred to the book or what he was doing to her with just a fingertip and his breath, warm against her skin. She lifted her gaze to his, but with his lids half-closed, she couldn't read his expression. Then he lowered his head, and she understood.

*He might be a killer.*

The thought should have turned her cold, should have brought out her instincts of self-preservation. But she'd regretted the interruption, for many reasons, that had stopped him from kissing her the first time they'd met. Only a day ago, yet he was as familiar to her as if she'd known him a lifetime....

She wanted no regrets this time. She wanted just one kiss to satisfy her curiosity. Then she'd push him away, and she would finally get some answers out of him. But the first answer she wanted was whether he tasted like her soul remembered.

She tilted her chin, lifting her lips to his.

He'd never felt this before—his *own* emotions—as he brushed his mouth across hers. Passion flicked through him, sending the blood rushing through his veins. He tunneled his fingers into the silky strands of blond hair, holding her head still as he deepened the kiss. He parted her lips with the pressure of his, then slid his tongue inside her mouth. To taste. To tease.

She murmured. He stilled, ready to stop if she was protesting. But the murmur turned to a moan, and she stepped closer, pressing her body against his. Despite her tall, slender build, her breasts were full, her hips soft. He slid his hands from her face, over her shoulders to her waist. And he kept kissing her as if she was the air he needed to breathe.

And she kissed him back just as desperately, her hands clutching at his shoulders, then his back, pulling him as close as they could be without being joined.

If only he could feel what she felt…

Every other time he'd been with a woman, he'd felt her desire, her pleasure, but with Alaina, he felt only the heat of his own passion as it flushed his skin. He felt only the urgency of his own need as his body throbbed. He'd never wanted anyone the way he wanted her.

Kissing wasn't enough. He had to touch her.

His fingers tangled around the belt of her robe, tugging it loose so that her lapels parted. Then he finally tore his mouth from hers, gasping for breath, and slid his lips down her throat.

She arched her neck and moaned. Until he moved lower, over the delicate curve of her collarbone to the slope of her breast. Her hands, which had clutched at him moments before, pushed at his chest, shoving him back.

That was when he noticed the faint white ridge of a jagged scar puckered over her heart. He staggered back a foot, unable to comprehend what he was seeing, besides her beauty. And God, she was beautiful, all sensual curves and silky skin… but for that scar that marred the perfection.

"I—I thought none of his victims survived," he murmured, his head pounding with confusion.

Her hands shook as she jerked the robe together and refastened the belt, tightly cinching her waist. "I'm not a victim."

"Not now," he agreed. No one could mistake Agent Paulsen for a victim. "What happened? When were you attacked?"

She met his gaze, the emotion in her eyes unfathomable.

He was not unfazed by the irony. The one person with whom he actually wanted to empathize, he could not reach.

"I was born with this scar," she said, stroking her fingers over the satin that covered the mark. "My parents took me to all kinds of specialists trying to explain it. Heck, they even got divorced over it because my father couldn't accept what my mother believes."

"What does your mother believe?" he asked, muscles clenching in his stomach. He knew… He'd known it from the first moment she'd walked into his den. Hell, even before that—as she'd drawn nearer to his house.

"My mom believes that I brought this scar with me from a former life." She drew in a shaky breath. "So although I am not a victim in this life, I was in a previous life."

"Reincarnation?" he asked, as if he'd never heard or considered the concept before. Like her father, Trent struggled to accept the explanation even though it might prove the only answer. "That's what your mother believes. What do you believe, Alaina?"

Her fingers kept stroking the scar, absently now, as if the gesture was an old habit of hers. "It's the only thing that makes sense."

And that was what he was afraid of. "So do you know…about your other life? Do you remember it?"

"Not much," she admitted. "Just flashes. Images. You saw all those files on my desk?"

He nodded, remembering the pile. He understood her devotion to all those old cases now.

"You were right about it being personal for me. But it isn't because one of those victims had been my mother or sister or aunt. It's because *I* was once one of those twelve women."

"In another life?"

She nodded; then, her voice raspy with frustration, she added, "But I don't know which one."

He knew. After all this lifetime of struggling to accept the truth of his memories, the realization overwhelmed him. Just as she had lived before, so had *he*.

"You don't believe me," she said, her eyes wide with vulnerability.

He couldn't admit to the fear that had haunted him for twenty-nine years. He could barely accept it himself.

"Then explain this." She jerked her robe open, baring her breasts. "Explain how I could have gotten a scar like this and lived?"

He closed his eyes, shutting out her beautiful body, shutting out the feelings only she had been able to draw from him. His body ached with wanting hers. He'd had other women, so many other women, but he'd always felt their passion, their pleasure. And even though his body had found release in theirs, he had never really experienced the passion or the pleasure himself. But he knew he could with Alaina.

Only Alaina.

"It's not from this life," she insisted, her voice

cracking with her desperation to make him believe.

He didn't need convincing. Not anymore. Not after having met her. But, reeling from the revelations, he couldn't deal with his own feelings, let alone hers.

So he forced his desire under control; he couldn't finish what he'd started with that kiss. Not yet. Curling his hands into fists so he wouldn't reach for her, he stepped around her and headed toward the door.

Alaina resisted the urge to grab him and plead for him to stay with her. She had done that once already, and the begging hadn't convinced her father to stay. Dear old Dad had still rejected her, unable to accept everything she was and once had been.

"You think I'm crazy," she said, regretting her admission. No one but her parents knew about the reincarnation theory. And she should have kept it that way. The only other people she'd discussed reincarnation with had no idea of her true identity; she was only a screen name on a website blog.

But she had thought Trent Baines, of everyone

she'd met in this lifetime, would understand. Because she was certain that they had once known each other in another life. Intimately. And those feelings, like the memories that weren't hers, had rushed over her when he'd kissed her. She'd wanted him like she had never wanted another man: passionately, almost obsessively.

Trent stopped at the door, his hand wrapped around the knob. He didn't turn back to her. He didn't deny that he believed her to be crazy.

"You're not going to the director, are you?" If he told the director they had an unstable agent working for the Bureau, he'd ruin her. Dread clutched at her. Her job was everything, not because she particularly wanted to be an investigator but because she wanted—she needed—the truth.

"I'll deny it," she warned him. "If you tell anyone what I told you, I'll deny it. I'll say that you made it up, just like one of your books."

"You're the one who told me that I'm not writing fiction," he reminded her. "And they would only have to see the scar, Alaina, to know that there's more to your story than you're telling."

"And what aren't you telling?" she asked. "You never answered my questions about your books, how you got so many of those details from the case files."

Maybe it wasn't the way she'd hoped; maybe it wasn't the same way she had. Hell, maybe she was crazy to think they had ever meant anything to each other. "Did the director feed you information?"

He shook his head. "He didn't need to. I knew. I just knew…"

Her breath backed up in her lungs. "Oh, my God. You, too? You remember…?"

He turned the knob and pulled open the door.

"Wait," she implored him. "Please stay." She had never met, in person, anyone who'd experienced the things she had, who had memories that were not hers.

"I can't stay." He uttered the words as if they caused him physical pain, as if it hurt him to leave her.

Or did it hurt him to remember? Was that why he was so anxious to go?

"Please," she said, burying her pride. "I want

to talk to you. I have so many questions for you."
So much she wanted to learn about him…and
about herself.

"Read the rest of the book," he advised. "It
may give you the answers you're looking for."
And he walked out, closing the door behind
him.

Would the book give her the answers he
couldn't? Or just wouldn't? If he believed, too,
why didn't he want to talk to her? What didn't
he want to tell her?

# Chapter 7

He loved her.

That was why he couldn't let her go back to her husband. Not like he had all the times before. No other woman would satisfy his desire. He'd tried so many times to find substitutes. But she was the one...

The only one...

Her lips brushed his in a soft kiss. A goodbye kiss. Only she didn't know yet how final this goodbye was. Not until his hands closed around her throat. As he exerted pressure, her eyes widened with shock and fear. And realization.

*"You know," he said. "You finally know who I am."*

*The Thief of Hearts.*

*He had taken her body so many times, but she'd refused him her heart. Refused to leave her husband. Despite the little time and attention the man gave her, she still loved him.*

*"And now you know you loved the wrong man," he said as she clawed at his wrists, trying to free herself. But she would never be free of him, any more than he would ever be free of her.*

*She couldn't scream; she couldn't even gasp for breath. He stole that from her first. Her eyes, such a deep penetrating green, rolled back in her head, and her tense body relaxed, sagging against him.*

*He rolled her onto her back, then he reached inside the drawer of the bedside table and pulled out the knife. "You wouldn't give me your heart, so I'm going to take it." Like he'd taken the hearts of all those other women.*

*But they hadn't been her. Their hearts had meant nothing to him. They had meant nothing to him.*

*Those women meant more to her husband,
more than she did, as he had neglected her in
order to find their killer. And the idiot had never
realized that he already knew the killer, that he
was a man he trusted, a man he called friend.
A man he would never suspect until it was too
late.*

*For her.*

*And him.*

*He waited until she regained consciousness,
until her lashes fluttered and her eyes opened.
He needed her to see. To know...*

*His hand shook as he gripped the familiar
handle. He dragged a breath deep into his lungs,
bringing forth all his passion. And he plunged
the knife deep into her chest.*

*Hell, maybe it was too late for all of them.
Maybe it was time to end it....*

Her hands shaking, Alaina set aside the pages
she'd just read. *He* had killed her?

Is that what would have happened had Trent
Baines stayed? Would she have awakened after
making love with him to another new life because
he'd taken this one, too?

He had told her to read the rest of it, but as

she flipped through the papers left in the box, she found only a couple more chapters. He hadn't given her the ending. But she didn't need to read the pages to know how the story—and her life— would end. Just as it had before.

Badly…

"She knows," he told the empty room. "She knows now who she is."

Satisfaction filled him. Finally. She knew the truth. This time would she choose the right man? Would she choose life over death?

He had hope that in this life she was smarter than she'd been in the past. This time she would willingly give her heart to the right man. She would finally love *him*.…

This was how he dealt…

Locking himself away in the fortress he'd found in northern Michigan. Locking himself away from other people's emotions. Locking himself away in case he posed a threat. In case he was the reincarnated Thief of Hearts.

The doors rattled, but the lock held. Trent ignored the intrusion and continued to stare out the window, over the fresh green treetops on the hillside.

A heavy fist lightly rapped and Dietrich called out, "Mr. Baines?"

His jaw clenched tightly; he didn't respond.

"Do you not wish to be disturbed?"

He was disturbed, deeply disturbed. Anyone who read his novels knew that. Alaina knew that. So why had she made the trek back up to the estate, to him?

The knocking turned to pounding. "Trent! Let me in," Alaina demanded. "We need to talk!"

If he remained silent, Dietrich would send her away, knowing that he was too immersed in his writing to tolerate any interruption. But he wasn't immersed. Behind him, on the desk, the laptop screen had gone black. He hadn't touched the keys since turning it on. He had no desire to write.

No desire for anything or anyone but her.

"Don't touch me!" she yelled out, the anger in her voice drawing Trent from the window.

He pulled open the pocket doors to witness her dropping Dietrich to his knees. The man fell heavily onto the hardwood floor. Color flushed his face. With anger or embarrassment, Trent could not tell; the man had never revealed any hint of emotion before.

Agent Paulsen could definitely take care of herself. Would she be able to protect herself from him?

"Why are you here?" he asked.

"Because we need to talk." The vulnerability was gone from her voice now, as it and her eyes were steady with determination.

"Mr. Baines?" Dietrich asked, regaining his feet with a grimace and groan. "Do you want me to show her out?"

Trent laughed. "I don't think you could if I wanted you to," he teased the other man. "It's fine. I'll see Agent Paulsen."

He'd seen her all night, the image of her naked body chasing away his sleep. He had been a fool to leave her with just a kiss when he'd needed so much more. He'd needed to lose himself inside her.

Today another of her dark suits hid the curves of her shapely body and the holster holding her gun. Unlike last night, when her hair had flowed around her shoulders, she'd clipped it up off her neck again. She wore another high-necked sweater, and now he understood why. To hide her scar...

Without so much as an apologetic or even reproachful glance at Dietrich, she stepped inside the den. Under her arm, she carried the box Trent had had his employee deliver to her.

He nodded at Dietrich, dismissing him, before he closed the doors. Now she was locked inside with him. To keep his distance from her, because he didn't trust himself not to shove her up against the wall and take her passionately, violently, he walked around his desk and dropped into the chair behind it.

"You told me to finish reading it," she said, her voice sharp with anger as she dropped the box next to his laptop, "but you didn't give me the rest of it. The ending's missing."

"It's not written yet," he admitted.

"Then why did you give the beginning to me?" she asked, her brow furrowed in confusion.

"You got yourself assigned to those cold cases," he said, remembering his dinner conversation with the director last night. "You've pored through all those files, looking for answers."

"Looking for a killer," she insisted.

"You weren't looking just for the killer," he said. "You were looking for yourself."

"You do believe me?" she asked, her voice soft with wonderment.

A twinge of sympathy struck him. Her own father hadn't believed her. After her dad's rejection, Trent doubted that she had trusted anyone else with her secret. "Yes, Alaina, I believe you." He pushed his hand through his hair and sighed. "But I don't want to believe you."

"But you know," she said. "You know it's the only explanation that makes sense." She planted her hands on his desk and leaned across it, her eyes narrowed as she studied him.

This was probably her interrogation face, the one that made suspects squirm with fear until they confessed all. A grin tugged at Trent's mouth that she'd used it on him. Because it only turned him on…

Hell, she didn't have to do anything to turn him on. The minute she got close, his body hardened, his heart pounded and his skin flushed with heat—all with desire for her. An image flashed through his mind—not of the past but of the future, of him throwing the computer and the box onto the floor and taking her atop his desk. His aching body driving into hers as they both sought release, fulfillment…

Her breath caught, her eyes widening as if she'd read his mind, and she jerked away from him.

"You know," he tossed her words back at her. "You know what I want…and you want it, too."

She shook her head and claimed, "I only want answers."

He grinned again, tempted to prove her a liar. All it had taken was one kiss last night. One kiss and passion had overcome whatever doubts or fears she might have had about him. But passion couldn't overcome *his* doubts and fears.

He sighed and commiserated. "You've been searching for answers your whole life."

Her eyes glistening with a hint of tears, she nodded. "Most kids grow up trying to figure out who they *are*. I spent my adolescence and now my adulthood trying to figure out who I *was*."

"Alaina…"

Her fingers trembled as she touched the

pages of the galley. "This is who I was, isn't it? Her?"

"I think so…" He knew it. To the depths of his old soul, he knew it.

If only he could be as certain about who he had been in their former life. Then maybe he wouldn't have spent this life afraid of that person.

"But those files," she said, her voice cracking with frustration, "I went over and over those files, and there was no mention of her. Anywhere."

"That was why you never figured it out," he said. "That was why you never connected with any of those other victims. You weren't one of those twelve women."

Her breath shuddered out in a ragged sigh. "I was *her*.…"

He couldn't feel what she felt, but he could see it all on her beautiful face: the disappointment, the disgust, the guilt.

"It was all my fault."

Trent shook his head. "No, it was his. He was the killer."

"But I—" She grimaced, her disgust evident again. "But the woman I was had an affair with him. She cheated on her husband with his friend, with a killer...." She pushed her fingers into her hair, tugging several pale blond locks loose of the clip at her nape.

"He started killing before she slept with him," he reminded her. She had claimed that she'd read all his books; like those files in her office, there had been no mention of her until this one—the last one.

"But she was his motivation," she said. "His inspiration. He killed women who looked like her, with red hair and green eyes."

"She was his obsession." And having met Alaina, having experienced the power and passion of this connection in the present, Trent almost understood. "It wasn't her fault that he was a killer."

"Still, she shouldn't have..." Her throat rippled as she swallowed hard. "She shouldn't have cheated on her husband."

"She was lonely," he said, reminding her of what he'd written, and what she had lived. "He gave her the attention her husband wasn't giving her."

"Her husband was the detective assigned to

those murders," Alaina said. "She should have understood that he had to stop the killer."

"And he should have understood that she needed him." More than his attention, she had needed his protection.

"Why do you keep defending her?" she asked, her brow furrowed with confusion, her voice sharp with frustration.

He sighed and admitted, "Because I loved her."

Her breath caught as her eyes widened. "Of course, you were the detective, Elijah Kooiyer. You had to be. That explains the accuracy of the procedural part of your books."

"Then I was a fool." But he'd prefer to have been a fool to a killer.

"I don't understand...."

"He neglected her. That made him a fool," he said. "That and having been friends with a killer. Why did he never figure it out? Why did he never get that those other women, all those victims, looked like his wife, that she was the object of the killer's obsession?"

Her eyes widened with surprise and awe. "I

don't understand how you remember so much," she said, "and I only have these flashes."

Trent shrugged, but he couldn't shake off the guilt, which was probably the reason those memories clung to him so vividly. "I don't know. Like you, they came in flashes, too. For years, just little flashes, little things that set off that sense of…"

"Déjà vu?"

"Yeah." He chuckled. "My parents thought I was crazy. Moody. Weird. I spent all my time alone."

But he'd had another reason for that—survival. Even now, as an adult, he couldn't deal with everyone else's emotions. As a kid, he had reeled under the pressure. And had nearly cracked. "But then, my freshmen year of college I took a creative writing course. And as I wrote, the memories became more vivid. It just flowed out of me. I didn't know, for sure, that any of it was real…until you came to me. And then I looked through those files last night…"

It had only taken him a glance at each to recognize the scene from a book. "My first book was published ten years ago," he said. "What took you so long to find me?"

"I had no idea what exactly had caused the scar. Those flashes of memory weren't clear enough for me to understand what had happened… besides my death," she explained. "It wasn't until after I joined the Bureau and started working cold cases that the memory became clearer."

He rubbed his eyes, wishing it could all go away, wishing he remembered none of it. But her.

"In all those files," she said, "there was no mention of the detective's wife, no report of her murder."

"I guess her body was never discovered. Like you said, there was nothing in those files—not even a mention of why the detective stopped working the case." And he'd looked through those folders carefully, trying to find anything to ease his dread.

She lifted a hand, then dropped it back to her side. "Why wouldn't there have been something…?"

He shrugged. "I don't know. Maybe those memories aren't really memories at all. Maybe they're not real." He'd hoped for so many years that they weren't.

"We both know that's not true." She touched her knuckles to her chest where, beneath her sweater, the scar marred the perfection of her silky skin. "The only thing we don't know is how and why the killing ended thirty years ago."

"Her body may not have been found, but she was killed. And once his obsession was gone…" He'd had no reason to kill anymore.

"Then why did the killing start again?" she asked.

He pushed his chair back from the desk, stood and turned toward the window. Fog had rolled in around the hilltop, adding to the seclusion of his fortress.

"Or do you know?" she asked.

He shook his head even though he had a feeling that it had started up for the same reason it had last time. Because of her…

"But you know so much," she said. "And if you really never saw those files until yesterday…"

"I didn't." And he wished he hadn't ever looked at them, that he hadn't confirmed that his nightmares had been someone else's living hell.

"Then your memories are very vivid." She came around the desk to stand beside him. Her arm bumped against his as she stepped closer.

But he couldn't look at her; he didn't want her to see what he was afraid he saw when he looked in the mirror. The soul of a killer.

"Your memories are real," she said, "not just flashes like mine. Hell, you even knew his motive. You knew the reason he took their hearts. He wanted their love. Her love."

And there was only one way he could know that... Only one way that memory could be his...

His stomach clenched with dread. And fear.

"You must know who he is and why he stopped," she insisted. She reached back to his desk, and her fingernails tapped his laptop. "You have to write the ending."

"I can't." He pushed his hand through his hair, grasping at the strands. "I've already missed my deadline. That's probably why my editor told you how to find me. He's pissed that the book is late."

"He wasn't happy when I talked to him," she agreed. "But he didn't want me to bother you.

I had to threaten him before he gave up your location."

"You threatened him?" he asked, amused at her persistence. "Why?"

"I had to find you," she admitted. "Your books were the first lead I'd found on the case until…"

"Another woman was murdered." His amusement faded. She hadn't sought him out as a fan, or because of what they might have once meant to each other.

"We have to stop him before anyone else gets hurt," she said, her voice breathy with urgency. "You have to write the ending."

"I can't," he said again, surprised that she referred to the killer as someone else, as someone other than him. He wished he could be as convinced as she that he'd been the cop instead of the killer.

"What are you saying?" she asked. "That you can't remember, that you can't write? Are you blocked?"

"No," he said. He only wished he was. "I can remember. I just don't want to."

A soft sigh of realization slipped through her

parted lips. "You're afraid of what you might find out."

"I'm afraid that I am—that I was," he amended his confession, "the Thief of Hearts."

## Chapter 8

"Oh, my God..." Her breath backed up in her lungs. "I—I hadn't..."

"Yes, yes, you had." He turned to her, finally, his green eyes full of torment as he met her gaze. "That's what brought you here. You read those books, and you suspected that I was the killer."

He stepped closer to her, but before he could touch her, she stepped back, out of his reach. Her action had been involuntary, though.

"See," he pointed out, "even now, maybe even more than before, you suspect me."

"But you're not," she said. He couldn't be—not

with how she felt about him. She hadn't backed
away out of fear. She had backed away because
when he was too close, her skin tingled and
her pulse quickened. And she wanted him. She
wanted the passion she remembered from that
other life. "You can't be."

"Because I was here when you got the call
the other day?" he asked. "We were both there
when the coroner told you the woman had been
dead for twenty-four hours." He gestured out the
window, at the fog-enshrouded hillside. "You
know I have a helicopter. It sits on a helipad right
on the roof of this house. I can come and go
quickly."

"Do you want me to suspect you?" Alaina
wondered, her pulse quickening now with the
fear she'd had yet to feel for him.

"The director speaks highly of you," he shared.
"You're a good agent. Smart. You should suspect
me." He pushed a hand through his hair, setting
the dark golden strands on end. "*I* suspect me."

She reached out, needing to comfort him as
much as she needed him. Her fingertips slid
across the back of his hand. But he pulled away,

as if he couldn't bear her touch. "Why do you suspect yourself?"

"The things I know..." Now the torment was in his voice, in the rough timbre of his already deep tones. "How else could I know them? How could I know his motive? His relationship with her?"

"If you were the detective, you could have learned all this in the course of your investigation."

He snorted with derision. "That guy was an idiot. For years he worked this case. For years he found this guy's victims—women who looked just like his wife. And he never realized the killer was his friend?"

"I don't know," she murmured, wishing she could comfort him.

"This friend slept with his wife, killed his wife, and he had no idea." His voice vibrated with anger and resentment as he added, "He was too stupid to figure it out."

Now she understood the perspective from which he wrote his books, the reason for his disdain of law enforcement. From his perspective, the killer had been smarter than the cop.

It was her turn to defend the man she was certain she had loved despite how her past actions must have hurt him. "Maybe he was just too trusting to suspect the people he loved of betraying him." Like his wife had betrayed him. Could she have really been that woman? "That doesn't make him a bad investigator."

"Just a fool…"

She had been the fool to betray a good man. But in the end she had paid for her mistake with her life. "What happened to the detective?"

He shrugged. "I have no idea. I didn't even know for sure that he was a real person and not just a figment of my imagination."

"Until you saw the files," she said. "He has notes on that last case. But that's not really the last case. His wife's murder has to be the final one—even though her body must have never been found."

"I don't know." He expelled a ragged sigh of frustration. And guilt…

If he were really the man he feared he'd been, would he feel guilt? Would he feel anything?

Her perception of the serial killer had always

been that he'd been a soulless monster. He wouldn't have had a soul to go on to another life.

"Maybe there are more victims, more bodies that haven't been found," she mused aloud. Maybe he hadn't stopped killing at all. "Women disappear all the time and are never seen again, their bodies never found."

Maybe she needed to search through the missing-person records for more victims.

"He never hid any of the other bodies," Trent reminded her. "It was like he wanted them to be found, just like this last victim was found."

"You need to write the ending to this book," she urged him. "We need to know."

He shook his head. "You want to know. We don't need to. It won't change what already happened."

"No," she agreed. She couldn't go back to that life; she couldn't undo what she'd done. She could only vow not to make the same mistakes again. "It won't change what happened. But it might stop more women from getting killed. Penelope Otten didn't deserve to die."

"No," he agreed, his handsome face twisting into a grimace as if he could feel the pain the woman had endured before she'd died. "She didn't."

"Did you know her?" she asked, finally asking the questions the investigator in her should have been asking him. But that other life called to her—and her connection with him was stronger than her instincts as an agent.

"No," he said. "At least, not that I remember..."

And Vonner, despite his efforts to find a link between them, had found nothing but Trent's book in her apartment. Alaina had checked it herself, but it hadn't been signed. She wasn't even convinced that Penelope Otten had been a fan of his writing. Her other books had been self-help and romance; there'd been no other horror or even suspense novels. Had the killer brought it with him, trying to implicate Trent in her murder?

"Maybe her death has nothing to do with our past lives." Maybe it had more to do with the present, with someone finding an excuse for killing.

"It too closely matches those old murders," he pointed out. "The murders I write about. If this isn't him killing again, it's someone copying my books." He tipped his head back and groaned. "And either way, her death is my fault."

His frustration and self-loathing rushed over her as if the emotions were her own. Her breath caught at the unexpected intensity of those feelings. It was unusual for her to experience any feelings, even her own.

She'd been so caught up in her past life that she hadn't done much living of this one. She hadn't fallen in love. She'd told herself it was because of the scar, because it had been too hard to explain to those few boyfriends she'd had.

But she'd kept herself aloof not just in her personal life but her professional one, too. The director hadn't assigned her to cold cases just because she'd asked. She knew that she had a reputation for being unsympathetic and insensitive. And until today, she would have agreed.

But with Trent, she was too sensitive—to her feelings for him and now to his feelings. All the torment she'd glimpsed in the depths of his green eyes and heard in the gravel of his deep voice, she now felt. And she knew only one way to end it…for them both.

"Please," she begged him, "please, you need to write the rest. To end this again, you're going to have to find out what happened thirty years ago."

He expelled a ragged sigh. "You've been working these cases for a long time."

"Just a few years on those cases. But my whole life," she said, "I've been trying to find out who I was and what exactly happened to me."

"And now that you know…?"

She wished she didn't. With understanding, she said, "So that's why you'd rather not know which man you were—killer or hero."

"The detective was no one's hero," he insisted. "So many women died senselessly. And he hadn't even been able to protect the woman he loved."

"We're not those people anymore—those people we once were," she reminded him and herself.

He laughed. "We are. We have their memories. Their souls…"

But not their hearts. At least, not hers. The killer had taken hers. In her past life. In this life, she was afraid that she was going to give it to him willingly.

The frustration, the torment emanating from him to her, didn't ease. She reached out again, sliding her fingers across the back of his hand.

This time he didn't pull away. He turned his hand around and caught her fingers, entwining them with his. And the frustration changed, became sexually charged, as desire caught fire between them.

Too hot, too intense…

She felt hers and his.

And she was overwhelmed. Her knees weakened, and her head grew light. She swayed as blackness threatened to consume her, like the desire burning her up.

He caught her. His heart pounding in his throat, he swept her up in his arms. This woman who was so strong, this woman who'd dropped a man twice her size, had nearly collapsed. What the hell was wrong with her? "Are you all right?"

"I—I can feel you."

Cradling her with one arm, he slid his other along the delicate line of her jaw. "I can feel you, too."

She shook her head, weakly. "No, I can feel…
what you feel."

He would have laughed at the irony of her
being the one person whose emotions he could
not feel. But he understood how frightening that
first experience with empathy had been. And of
anyone's emotions, his were complicated and
conflicted as hell. But for what he felt for her…

"You want me," she said.

"Badly."

"So take me," she offered. "Just…take
me…"

"Alaina?" Hope sent his pulse racing. Could
she want him, too? "Are you sure?"

"I want you," she said. "I want to know…"

Who he was?

"What it was like," she clarified. "I want to
know what it was like between us. I only have
those images. I want the reality. I want to feel
you—and all the passion—in the present, not the
past."

"It may be too much," he warned her. Not
just for her, though. He worried it might be too
much for him. Their connection was already so
strong.

"I want to know, even if it's too much." She reached up, locking her arms around his neck and pulling his head down to hers.

He kissed her. Just a brush of his mouth across her sweet lips before he pulled away. No matter how much he wanted her, he wouldn't take her here, not on the desk or the floor or the narrow leather couch on one side of the room. His body throbbing with a need so intense it was painful, he carried her to the bookshelves and he knocked his elbow against the switch that slid them apart to reveal the doorway to the back stairs.

She wriggled, trying to regain her feet. "I can walk." Her breasts pushed against his chest, her hip rubbing against his abdomen.

He tightened his hold and climbed the narrow steps. Another press of a button and the back wall of the closet opened; he passed through its open door into the master bedroom.

She trembled against him, and his arms tightened even more. But then he forced his muscles to relax and he released her. She slid down his body, her thighs pressing against his, her hips arching against the erection that throbbed, almost painfully, behind the zipper of his jeans.

But he didn't know if she trembled out of fear or desire. "If you're afraid, you can leave."

And somehow he would force himself to let her go.

She didn't step away from him. She stayed close, so close that he felt the warmth of her breath as she released the laughter, which had actually been what had shaken her body. "I can't believe that you literally have secret passageways. This place is really a castle."

"It's a fortress," he admitted.

"To keep people out?" she wondered aloud, her gaze soft on his. "Or yourself inside?"

He shuddered now. She knew him so well. And still she wanted him?

"This is your last chance," Trent warned her, fisting his fingers into his palms so that he wouldn't grab her and pull her tightly against him. "This is your last opportunity to leave."

She shook her head. "You don't scare me."

"Then that makes one of us."

She laughed again, then she reached for him, her hands locking around the nape of his neck to pull his head down to her level. "And really kiss me this time. Kiss me like you kissed me last night."

He kissed her like a drowning man gasped for air, filling his lungs with the warmth of her breath, the sweetness of her desire for him. He felt it not in the way he experienced other people's emotions. He felt her feelings in the scrape of her teeth across his bottom lip, in the flirty forays of her tongue sliding inside his mouth, tangling with his.

She pulled away and staggered back a step, dazed, as she panted for breath. "The things you can make me feel with just a kiss…"

"It's what you make me feel," he said. "But you know what I'm feeling. You're experiencing it now, the force of my desire for you."

Obsessive desire? Did he dare do more than kiss her? Was this really her last chance to leave him before he wouldn't let her leave him ever again?

But then she reached for the buttons on her suit jacket, her fingers trembling as she undid them. She shrugged the jacket off her narrow shoulders and reached next for her holster. Her fingers steady now, Alaina held tight to the handle of her weapon.

He tensed, waiting for her to turn the barrel on him. Had this been her plan all along? Did she remember more than he had remembered? Did she already know he was the killer?

Maybe she hadn't come up here for answers. Maybe she'd come after him for revenge.

"Are you going to use that on me?" he asked, gesturing toward her gun.

She stared down at it, as if she hadn't realized she held on to it. Her eyes widened in surprise.

"Do you think you'll need it?" he asked, reeling from the flash of hurt over her doubts. But he couldn't blame her for doubting him when he doubted himself. "Do you think I'm going to hurt you?"

Or that he already had?

## Chapter 9

"I can feel what you feel," Alaina said, still stunned that she possessed that strange ability. "But I can't read your mind."

If only she could, then she would have the answers—all the answers—she sought. She would know if she was doing the right thing or making another mistake that would cost her *this* life.

"You don't need the gun," he assured her.

She didn't trust him, but she wanted him too much to listen to the voice of common sense that nagged at her conscience. Or maybe it was

Vonner's voice, gruff with all the suspicions he'd spewed about Trent Baines.

She'd called in sick to work today, the first day of work she'd missed since the vacation her mother had forced her to take a few years ago. Before Alaina had discovered the cold cases that coincided with the memory of her death.

Since then, she hadn't missed a day. Until now...

Maybe she was sick. She hadn't slept at all after reading those pages of his manuscript, after discovering who she'd been and what she'd done.

If only she knew for sure which man Trent Baines had been.

Her husband or her killer...

"I won't hurt you," he promised, his green eyes bright with a sincerity she felt as acutely as if it was her own, like the flash of hurt that had twinged in her chest when she'd first touched the handle of her gun. That had been *his* hurt—that she had doubted him.

But the doubts held tight to her. She'd known him such a short amount of time in this life.

Yet she felt as if she'd known him forever in

another. That it was just perfectly natural, and absolutely necessary, to make love with him. "Trent…?"

"I can't promise that I wasn't the one who hurt you," he admitted, "because I don't know."

And he didn't want to know. At the moment neither did she. She only wanted him.

His desire pumped through her veins, increasing the intensity of her own passion. Her fingers trembled as she set the holster, and her .45, onto the table beside the bed. It was mahogany, like his den, and like the king-size sleigh bed. And the dresser and the wainscoting beneath the striped wallpaper. The gun gone from her grasp, her decision made, she reached for the hem of her sweater.

He watched her, his green eyes darkening as his pupils dilated. His breath shuddered out as she lifted the light knit fabric. As she pulled the sweater over her head, the clip fell from her hair; it dropped to the floor with the sweater and her hair fell loose around her bare shoulders.

Impatience spurred his desire and hers. He dragged his black T-shirt over his head, mussing his hair even more than his hands had earlier. He reached next for the snap of his jeans, undoing it before dragging down the zipper.

Her bottom lip dropped, her breath drying its dampness, as she uttered an appreciative sigh. He was beautiful, from the sculpted muscles of his chest to the washboard abs that led to his waist. His lean hips jutted above his sagging jeans. Her heart pounded heavily. She had never wanted anyone with this intensity—not even the man with whom she'd made love in those brief flashes of old memories.

Was the intensity only because she felt his emotions in addition to her own? Her hands shook so violently she barely managed to unclasp her pants. The teeth of her zipper caught as she jerked it down. Then she wriggled out of the trousers, so that she stood before him in only her panties and bra. The lace and satin barely covered the slope of breasts or the curls between her thighs.

His breath shuddered out in a ragged sigh of appreciation. "You are so damn beautiful."

"And crazy," she said. "This is crazy…" But she couldn't stop now, even if he held her gun to her head.

But then he touched her and chased the last of her doubts away with the fire of his passion. Only his fingertip brushed across her skin, gliding down her throat, over her leaping pulse to the hollow between her breasts.

She shivered, goose bumps lifting along her arms and nape. But then his hand was there, tangling in her hair. He sifted his fingers through the strands and sighed. "So damn beautiful…"

Pressure built inside her, winding tight. "Touch me," she ordered him. "Really touch me."

His fingertip continued down her stomach to dip into her navel. Then lower it traveled, over her stomach to the lace of her panties. That finger flicked over the center of her desire, over the tight little nub.

Passion flowed through her, pooling low in her womb, centering on that nub that he flicked again, this time with his thumb. He pressed harder.

She parted her legs, giving him access, but he moved his hand back up her body and around her back. The clasp of her bra parted. Then he pulled the straps until they slipped down her arms and the cups fell away from her breasts.

Her nipples, peaked with the desire burning inside her, tilted toward him, begging for his attention.

But he touched her only with his gaze, sliding it over her. He didn't stop at the scar, like he had last night. It didn't turn him off again, like it had some men before him. Instead, he only glanced at it.

"You're teasing me," she complained.

"I'm savoring you," he corrected her, his voice rough with the desire she felt straining at his restraint, testing his control.

She wanted to test it, too. So she slid her hands over his chest. His heart beat fast and hard beneath her palm. Then her hands traveled lower, until her fingers dipped inside his open waistband. She reached beneath the elastic of his boxers and freed his erection. It leaped, throbbing with the intensity of his need.

A need that matched her own.

She leaned forward, so that the tips of her breasts touched his chest. The nipples rubbed against his hot skin. Soft hair stroked the sensitive points, and she arched her neck, a moan slipping free of her lips.

So he caught her off guard. His hands closed around her waist and he lifted her. Then he lowered her onto the mattress, and he followed her down, his body covering hers. His mouth found hers, biting gently at her lips until she opened them for his tongue. It slid in and out. But it wasn't enough. Neither was the brush of his chest against her breasts.

The pressure inside her built, so intense she writhed beneath him, rubbing her hips against his erection. But her panties, however flimsy the lace, separated them. And she wanted nothing separating them. Not any garment or any doubt.

She belonged here, in his bed, beneath him....

He slid his mouth from hers, across her cheek to her ear. "I'm going to make you scream," he warned her, his breath hot against her skin.

She shivered with fear and anticipation. Her teeth sank into her bottom lip, and she shook her head. "No..."

"I'm going to make you scream," he said again, his eyes glittering with intent. Then he lowered his mouth, sliding it over the curve of one breast before his lips closed around the nipple. His tongue flicked across the point.

She whimpered as the pressure tightened her muscles, and she pressed her thighs together. But his hand was there, forcing them apart as he cupped her heat. His tongue continued to tease, flicking back and forth across her nipple as his fingers eased under the elastic of her panties and then inside her. His thumb rubbed the nub again.

His fingers moved, in and out. But it wasn't enough; release eluded her. She bit harder on her lip, but another moan slipped out.

He closed his teeth around her nipple and tugged. She arched, lifting her breast against his mouth and her hips against his hand. An orgasm ripped through her, taking off the edge but not releasing that pressure. Then he moved his mouth from her breast, his tongue following the path his finger had taken earlier.

He tugged the panties off her now, lifted her legs and hooked them over his shoulders. Then he buried his face between her thighs. His mouth moved over her, his tongue flicking back and forth over her clit like it had her nipple. But he didn't neglect her breasts; his hands cupped their fullness, his palms pressing against her nipples.

She shifted against the bed and tugged at his hair. But she didn't pull him away. She held him to her. He slid his tongue inside her, lapping at her. She arched against his mouth and hands, and a scream of frustration tore from her throat. Then the frustration eased as another orgasm shuddered through her. And she screamed at the intensity of the pleasure.

But then she felt his frustration, his overwhelming desire for her, so acute it bordered on pain. He pulled away and kicked off his jeans. Then he dragged open the top drawer of the bedside table and pulled out a condom. His hand shook as he ripped it open, then rolled it onto the impressive, pulsing length of his erection. He reached for her again and pushed her legs apart. Then, with a passion edging toward frenzy, he drove inside her.

She spread her legs wide and wrapped them around his waist, trying to take all of him. Trying to take him deep. But he was too much, too big...

Too intense.

Every feeling of his pummeled her, increasing her own desire. She grasped his shoulders, clawing at the sinewy muscles. Then she rose up and kissed him, sliding her tongue into his mouth. He held it with his lips, before letting her pull away and pant for breath. Her lungs burned, needing air. But she needed him more.

He lowered his head and tugged a nipple into his mouth. As he stroked his tongue over the point, he withdrew his penis and stroked the moist tip of it over the nub of her femininity—before sliding inside her again.

She stretched, accepting more of him, taking him deeper. With each thrust she came closer to finally releasing the pressure he'd built inside her. Passion dampened her skin, making it slide against his as their bodies joined.

His passion burned inside her, hot and intense. He was close, too.

As he thrust, he reached between them, rubbing his thumb across her most sensitive spot.

And finally the pressure broke. An orgasm slammed through her, so intense that she screamed his name, her throat burning from the force and volume of her cry. He thrust again and again and again, extending her orgasm even as he climbed toward his own.

She felt his control snap, felt the red haze of passion overcome him as he thrust once more, then came. A groan tore free from his throat, raw and primal.

Her lungs still laboring for breath, she dropped back on the mattress and gasped. "That was..." Like nothing she had ever experienced before. In this life, or maybe even her last. "That was incredible."

He grinned that arrogant grin that had fascinated even as it infuriated her. "You screamed," he reminded her as he flopped onto his back, slid his arm around her and clutched her against his side. "Twice..."

She shook her head, but her lips curved into a weak smile of admission. Drained now by their passion, she rested her head against his chest. Her eyes, the lids so heavy, threatened to close. But she fought against sleep. She had so many things she wanted to ask him, so many things she needed to know about them now...and them back then.

Had he remembered anything more?

She'd expected to see again the images that had flickered behind her lids ever since their first meeting. But she had seen nothing. She'd been too busy feeling.

Even now, as her eyes closed, she saw only the sweet black of oblivion. No images of her past life or death. Or of the man she had loved and betrayed. She forced her eyes open and stared up at his face.

Stubble darkened the line of his strong jaw and clung to the hollows beneath his sculpted cheekbones. He was so handsome, so beautiful....

"Why did you cover your face for the picture on your book jacket?" she wondered aloud. "Were you afraid that if they knew what you looked like, you would have hoards of adoring fans stalking you?"

His mouth quirked into a self-deprecating grin. "Given what I write, the last thing I worried about was adoring fans. But I did worry about my privacy."

"Since you live in a fortress, I kind of figured out that you value your privacy," she admitted, then pressed her fist to her mouth to stifle a yawn.

"Go to sleep," he told her, his hand stroking her back and shoulder. "Get some rest before I wake you up and make you scream again."

She shivered with anticipation and a resurgence of desire. "I—I need to get back to Detroit," she said even though she didn't want to leave his bed or his arms. "I shouldn't have come up here, but I had to know..."

"Who you were?"

"About us," she said. "I kept seeing us together, but it wasn't *us*."

"Me, too," he said. "The woman looked different but I knew it was you. If only I knew for sure who I was...."

"You will," she said, "when you finish your book. That's another reason I should go. So you're not distracted from writing." But she yawned again, her sleepless night overwhelming her with bone-deep weariness.

"You can't make that long drive until you get some sleep," he said. "These roads can be treacherous when you're wide-awake and alert. You need to get some rest."

She wanted to, but those last doubts niggled at her. Dare she fall asleep in his arms, in his bed? Would she ever wake up again?

## Chapter 10

*He held her heart in his hands, blood oozing between his fingers. It was almost as if it beat yet, as if she lived. But she didn't, not anymore. He had seen to that.*

*Killing her had been the hardest thing he'd ever done. But there was no way he could have let her leave him again. No way. He loved her too much to ever let her go.*

*And now she would forever be with him. He would forever hold her heart in his hands.*

His hands shaking, Trent slammed the laptop closed with such force the plastic cracked. He picked it up, tempted to hurl it out the window onto the trees and rocks below. But then he dropped it back onto his desk. It wouldn't matter if he threw it out. The memories would keep coming.

His memories. He had to have been the Thief of Hearts. Nothing else made any sense. How else could he have known exactly what the man had done and why?

Because of *her*...

He glanced toward the bookshelf that concealed the back stairwell. The urge to slide those shelves aside and climb the steps to her propelled him across the room. But he couldn't. He couldn't go up to where she slept in his bed.

He couldn't touch her again knowing that he had to have been the man who killed her. If they made love again, he might become as obsessed with her as he had been in their other life. Loving her might bring forth all his old tendencies...

For murder.

He closed his eyes, remembering the crime scene from two days ago. The blood spattered across the walls and the back cover of his book. The blood on his hand...

Was it already too late?

* * *

A scream burned the back of her throat, but Alaina couldn't utter it. She couldn't escape the nightmare.

Finally she fought her way free of the hold of the dream and jerked awake, her hand pressed to the scar over her heart. The fear and horror clung to her. But were the emotions hers or his? Alone in the bed, she clutched the tangled sheets to her body and visually searched the room for him. Dawn's light streaking through the blinds dispelled the shadows.

Dawn?

Images flashed through her mind, images of the past night instead of a past life. Trent making love to her. Again and again they had reached for each other, unable to get enough. And the sensations, the emotions, had been more intense each time they had made love.

The emotions pummeling her now were different, frightening. So much guilt and regret...

Despite what they'd done, she had no regrets. She'd wanted to know how it would feel to make love with him, if it would measure up to the passion in her flashes of memory. So the guilt and regret had to be all his.

What had he done?

She had to find him. Her hands shaking, she pulled on her clothes, then reached for her holster. In addition to the gun, it had a compartment for her phone and wallet. The phone beeped, probably from a low battery, but when she glanced at it, she noted the little envelope icon indicating a voice mail. She couldn't deal with it now. She had to find Trent.

Although she patted the walls of the inside of the walk-in closet, Alaina couldn't find the switch for the secret panel that hid the back stairwell. So she used the door to the hall and found the grand staircase that opened onto the two-story foyer.

Her footsteps echoed throughout the cavernous hall as she headed toward his den. But before she could reach for the doors, someone grabbed her arm.

"Mr. Baines does not want to be disturbed," Dietrich warned her.

Heat burned her face, but despite her embarrassment over sleeping with someone she had once considered a murder suspect, she turned toward Trent's assistant. "So he's in there?"

His wide shoulders lifted in a shrug. "I don't know. The doors are locked, and he won't answer my knock. Or any of my calls."

"The doors are locked, so he has to be inside, then," Alaina murmured, needing to convince herself that he was in his den and not out doing something he regretted.

Like killing someone...

Dietrich shrugged again. "I don't know. This place has all these secret passageways. Sometimes I think that he has locked himself away to write, but then I'll hear the helicopter take off."

"Did you hear it?" she asked, alarm shortening her breath. Had Trent left her alone?

His assistant shook his head. "I don't know. I don't think so..."

"Do you know where he goes," she asked, "when he just takes off?"

"I know better than to ask Mr. Baines too many questions," Dietrich told her.

"Would he fire you if you did?"

He shook his head again. "He just wouldn't—doesn't—answer me."

She'd experienced that frustration herself when she had talked to him the first time just a couple of days ago. What in the hell had she been thinking to make love with him? Maybe the guilt and regret was hers, after all.

"He can be evasive," she agreed.

"Actually, I don't think he knows the answers himself," Dietrich admitted. "I think he gets so lost in his writing that it's like he blacks out. He remembers nothing of what he's done…"

In this life.

Was that because he remembered his other life too vividly? Had he been the killer then… and now?

Her doubts struck him like a blow, and Trent winced. Finally he connected with her, feeling her emotions. And the first thing he experienced was her suspicion of him.

He'd warned her; he should have been happy she had finally heeded that warning. It was better that she didn't trust him because he sure as hell didn't trust himself.

Yet he couldn't stop himself from opening the doors to see her again. Not the doors to the hall. She was no longer there. Instead, he pushed apart the bookshelves and climbed the back stairs to the bedroom. He stepped out of the closet to find her down on her hands and knees on the floor, looking under the bed.

He twirled her key chain around his finger. "Looking for these?"

"You took my keys?" she asked with a little nervous catch of breath. "I thought they fell out of my pocket."

"No, I took them," he admitted. He hadn't wanted her to leave. Hell, it was too late. He was already obsessed with her, already so connected that he couldn't let her go.

"Why?" She reached beneath her coat, no doubt going for her gun.

Instead of fear, pride and relief filled him. She was too smart to take chances, despite what they'd done the night before.

He admitted, "I wanted to know when you left."

"You didn't want to stop me from leaving?" she asked, her eyes narrowed as she studied his face.

"No," Trent lied, and she probably knew it.

She probably felt it, like he had finally felt her emotions. "So are you leaving?"

She nodded. "I have to get back to work."

"They don't know where you are," he guessed. Or the overprotective Agent Vonner would have already been pounding down his door.

"I called in sick yesterday." And with the color drained from her face, she looked sick. Sick with guilt over what they'd done. Her fingers trembling slightly, she took the keys from his hand.

Her phone beeped, and she reached for it. "They keep calling."

"I'm surprised you got a signal at all up here," he said. "It's usually pretty hit-and-miss."

"It's secluded up here," she agreed with a shiver as she studied the ID screen of her phone.

"Answer it," he advised her.

With a sigh, she lifted the cell to her ear and clicked a button. "Agent Paulsen."

*Agent.* At the moment, standing next to the tangled sheets of the bed where they had made love all night, she didn't feel as though she deserved the title.

"Alaina, where the hell have you been?"

"Sick," she lied to her partner.

"Where have you been?" Vonner asked again. "I stopped by your place yesterday. A couple of times. Your car wasn't in the lot."

So he'd found her address. He must have hacked into the personnel files. The first time she'd met the young agent she had picked up on his resourcefulness—and his ambition. "You must have missed my SUV," she insisted.

"That's what I thought," he admitted, "so I still went to your door."

"I wasn't answering it."

"Or your phone," he said. "The second time I didn't knock. I just let myself in."

"You broke in?"

"I wanted to figure out why the hell you'd gone off in the middle of a murder investigation and where you were—to make sure you were all right." His voice rough with disapproval, he asked, "Are you with *him?*"

"It's not any of your business where I am or who I'm with," she said.

"It is if you're working the case on your own," Vonner said.

She had no connection to Vonner, but she didn't have to in order to hear his anger. "I'm not…" But she should have been. "You don't need to worry about the case."

"I'm worried about you," he admitted. "Even more so now. There's been another murder here."

"When?"

His sigh rattled the phone. "Rosenthal figures T.O.D. was sometime last night."

She glanced at the bed, remembering all those many, many times she and Trent had made love. She remembered lips brushing across lips, clinging, tongues tangling, skin sliding over skin as his body joined hers over and over again.

Relief shuddered out of her; it couldn't have been him. "I'll be there as soon as I can." She clicked off the cell and turned to Trent, who watched her, his gaze narrowed on her face.

"Someone else died?" he asked, a muscle ticking beneath the dark gold stubble on his jaw.

She nodded. "So it couldn't have been you. You were here with me."

"I could have left last night," he pointed out, "after you fell asleep."

Why was he so determined for her to think

the worst of him? Because he thought the worst of himself.

"No, you couldn't have," she argued. "We didn't sleep much last night."

His breath escaped in a ragged sigh, then he acknowledged, "No, we didn't."

She glanced again to the bed, remembering everything they'd done to each other. Every kiss, every caress…

Pushing the new images from her mind, she stammered, "I—I have to leave."

"I'm going, too," he said.

"No, you can't," she said, horrified at the thought of him at another crime scene, showing up with her, in front of Vonner's disapproving face.

"The director says I can," he reminded her. "He's given me clearance."

"Why? And don't tell me it's just because Graves is a fan." Something else she doubted. "What do you have on him?"

"Seriously, nothing," he claimed. "He must think, because of the books, that I can help. That I can see something you might miss."

"I won't miss anything," she assured him, "once I get there."

"I'm going, too," he said again. "I'll either beat you there or you can ride with me."

Within minutes, they were on their way, the helicopter lifting off from the pad on the roof of Trent's fortress. Alaina's heart pounded hard with nerves as she watched the ground below, the treetops and the castle, getting smaller and smaller.

"Relax," he urged her, speaking directly in her ear through the headphones she wore, "and enjoy the ride."

She wouldn't relax until they found the killer. But she could take in the scenery. Like him at the controls, so arrogant in his confidence. Dark glasses concealed those compelling eyes. Sexy stubble darkened his strong jaw, and his hair appeared lighter in the sun shining through the mostly glass body of the copter. It looked as though he had run his fingers through it instead of a comb.

She wanted to run her fingers through the soft strands, like she had last night when she'd held his mouth to hers. She could taste him yet on her lips, her tongue....

She pulled her gaze away, refusing to be drawn to him again. Yet. Instead, she studied the landscape below them and glimpsed the hip roof of another building on the hillside. "Who lives there?"

"Just rats, probably," Trent answered, following the direction of her pointing finger to the rooftop. "That's an old barn on my property."

"All of this is yours?"

He turned to her, his gaze possessive. "Yes, it's all mine."

And Alaina was afraid that he was right.

She was all his....

## Chapter 11

The walls were thin—too thin—and tumultuous emotions flooded the crime scene. Trent's head pounded as he tried to process everything he was feeling. But there was fear. So much fear...

He closed his eyes, shutting out the broken furniture and blood-spattered walls, but he couldn't shut out those emotions that pummeled him. He gasped, fighting for breath. "She fought..."

"But he overpowered her," Alaina said, her voice cracking with emotion.

Hers were the only ones Trent couldn't feel right now. But he opened his eyes and studied her face. The color had drained from her skin as she studied the crime scene. There was so much blood....

"He's such a sick bastard," Trent said, choking for breath, like his latest victim had choked for breath. The son of a bitch hadn't strangled her to death, though. Like last time, he had waited for her to regain consciousness before he'd plunged the knife into her chest, into her heart.

Trent reeled from the agony and doubled over, clutching his hand to his chest.

"Are you all right?" Alaina asked, her voice soft with concern. Her fingers brushed gently over his arm, but even her touch couldn't distract him from the horror that gripped him.

A stronger feeling, darker and more violent, pushed out the pain and fear. For the first time Trent experienced the killer's emotions—his rage and hatred. And his frustration and resentment. Even though he'd killed, this murder hadn't satisfied him. This woman wasn't the one he had wanted to kill, the one he planned to kill.

Once again Alaina was that woman, the object of a killer's sick obsession.

She was going to be next....

"You're in danger," he warned her as the rage and hatred overwhelmed him.

"The killer's long gone," she assured him, her fingers tightening on his arm.

But the madman's feelings weren't gone. Trent couldn't shake them off. Nor could he shake off the feelings of the other residents of the apartment complex. Their fear over the murder in their midst. And their guilt. Had there been witnesses? People who'd heard her screams, her fight, but had not come to her aid?

Before they could deal with the guilt that would haunt them, Trent had to deal with it. All of it. The leftover emotions from the victim, the killer and the reluctant witnesses…

It was too much. He couldn't shut them out, so he shut down, letting the blackness of his soul overtake his mind, as well.

"Is he going to be all right?" Alaina asked the doctor, her heart beating fast and hard as she recalled Trent dropping to the floor and falling across the blood-soaked carpet where the victim's body must have lain before the coroner had taken her to the morgue in the basement of the federal building.

The doctor nodded, and Alaina's breath shuddered out with relief. She'd been so worried.

She had barely felt Trent's breath as she'd leaned over him, checking for his pulse. It had been so thready and weak, as if this life had been about to slip away from him, too.

"What happened to him?" she asked.

"Exhaustion," the E.R. doctor diagnosed. "I would guess he hasn't slept in days. Maybe longer..."

Guilt flashed through Alaina, but then she doubted he would have slept last night even if she hadn't invaded his fortress. And she doubted that exhaustion really had anything to do with his collapse.

She had nearly passed out herself when she'd felt his emotions the night before. And he had understood her reaction, probably because he was empathetic himself. Probably had always been. That was why he locked himself away from the world. He couldn't deal with all those emotions.

She hadn't felt anything he'd felt back at the crime scene. She'd only seen the emotions chase across his face, with grimaces of horror and pain.

And then the life had left him as he'd passed out cold.

"Can I see him?" she asked, needing the visual reassurance that he was all right.

"Of course," the doctor said. "Follow me."

She started forward, only to have a strong hand close around her arm and jerk her back.

"You're not going anywhere until we talk," Vonner said, his face flushed with anger. "Go ahead, Doc. She'll catch up with you later." He dismissed the young resident.

She'd forgotten Vonner was there in the waiting room with her. He had showed up as the ambulance had been pulling away from the crime scene, with Trent and her in the back. She'd ridden with him, unable to leave his side until the doctors had taken him back to the E.R. She'd been surprised that Vonner had followed them to the hospital. He hadn't said anything, just silently paced, while they'd waited for word on Trent's condition.

"I have to talk to him first," she said. "I have to find out what happened to him." Even though she was pretty certain she already knew. But she needed to know what he'd felt. Emotions weren't something that could be processed like the other evidence at a crime scene. It could be the missing piece they needed to form a clear picture of the killer.

"You have to talk to me first," Vonner insisted, "and explain to me what the hell you're doing."

She tugged, trying to free herself from his tight grasp. "I'll be right back—"

"And it'll be too late," he warned her. "I'll have gone to the director and reported you. I should have already talked to him when I found out you weren't really sick yesterday." He snorted in derision. "Then again, maybe you are, because you, of all people, should know better than to get involved with a murder suspect."

"You don't know what you're talking about," Alaina insisted even as heat rushed to her face as the memories of just how involved she'd gotten with Trent flashed through her mind.

Vonner laughed now, with bitterness instead of amusement. "You came with him. In his helicopter."

They hadn't landed on the roof of the apartment building. They'd taken a rental car from the hangar he'd rented at the airport. "How do you know where I was?"

"I traced the GPS in your cell," he admitted. "I know you were with him."

"Vonner—"

"Do you even know my first name?" he wondered aloud. He pulled her closer, so that her body pressed against his long, taut one. "Do you know anything about me?"

She knew his first name, but after everything that had happened, and her concern for Trent, she couldn't think of it. "I—I…"

"Vince. It's Vince, Alaina." He shook his head. "You've been holding me at arm's length, using work as an excuse, arguing that it wouldn't be professional for us to get involved." He wrapped an arm around her back, keeping her tight against him as he lowered his head.

But Alaina twisted away from him, disgusted at the thought of any man but Trent kissing her or touching her. "Vince—"

"How professional is it for you to take up with a murder suspect?" he asked.

"I haven't taken up with him."

"I know where you were," he reminded her.

"You weren't out sick. You were with him." He sighed and pushed a hand through his thick, dark hair. "But that is sick. How could you be with him, knowing what he might be?"

"You're wrong about him."

"You were the one who insisted he could still be the killer," he said, flinging her suspicions back at her.

"I've changed my mind."

"I haven't changed mine," he said. "If anything, his little freak-out at the scene only makes him look guiltier."

"He was with me last night. All night," she admitted since Vonner already knew. "At his estate. He couldn't have killed her." Unless he'd slipped away while she'd been sleeping...

He chuckled. "You say the words, but you don't believe them, Alaina. I can see the doubt in your eyes. You don't know for sure that it's not him. You don't really know anything about him."

"I do." She knew she hadn't slept long enough for him to have flown to Detroit, killed a woman and flown back to the U.P.

Vonner shook his head. "Damn, look at him.

Really look at him. Can't you figure out who he is?"

The Thief of Hearts? It wasn't who he was now, but she couldn't deny that he might have been.

"His manservant's Igor," Vonner explained. "He's Dr. Frankenstein, and you can bet that somewhere in that spooky castle he calls home, he's hiding a monster. I think it's inside him. And I don't want you there when the monster comes out."

She shook her head, refusing to believe the worst of Trent. "He's not a monster."

"Then how do you explain those books he writes?" he challenged her. "Even if you alibi him for this murder, he's still to blame. He started this all up again with those damn books!"

That was what Trent believed, too, and his guilt overwhelmed her. But was this killer really copying the murders in Trent's novels? Or had he just started killing again, exactly like he had killed before?

Just because Alaina and Trent lived new lives now didn't mean the killer did, too. He could be living the same life he had always lived—as the original and only Thief of Hearts.…

God, he'd thought she would be smarter in this life. She was a federal agent, for crying out loud. She should have been too smart to make the same mistakes she had in her past life.

"It's your fault," he raged at her, but she couldn't hear him. Even if she could, she wouldn't listen. Just like last time. "All those other women are going to have to die again because of you, Alaina, because…"

She'd fallen for the wrong man again. And since she would not willingly give him her heart, he would just have to take it, still beating, from her chest…

Just like last time.

## Chapter 12

"You shouldn't be here," she said as Trent followed her down the corridor leading to the morgue.

But he had to stick close to her; he knew now that there was someone out there who posed a greater threat to her life than he did.

"I'm fine," he assured her. As fine as he could be when he knew she was in danger. Again.

"You checked yourself out against doctor's orders," she reminded him, her voice sharp with disapproval.

He grinned, knowing his cockiness infuriated

and distracted her. "I don't like being told what to do."

Her lips remained in a tight line of disapproval and concern. "But you ripped out the IV before it was done, and you needed that."

Trent laughed. "An IV, no matter what the hell they put in it, is not going to help what's wrong with me. We both know that."

"Yes," she said as she stopped outside the door to Autopsy. "And that's why you shouldn't go in here. You fell to your knees when you were in there with the last victim. You experienced everything she felt last, didn't you?"

He didn't bother lying. "Yes."

"That's how you knew exactly what had happened to her and how she had died?" she asked, easily accepting what his own parents, not to mention countless school counselors and child psychologists, had failed to understand.

"Yes," he admitted. "How did you think I knew? Because I killed her?"

"I didn't know you then," she said, not bothering to deny her suspicions.

Trent appreciated her honesty. While she might have the same soul as the detective's wife, she was not the same woman. She would not betray him again. But he couldn't be certain that, if he had the soul of the killer, he wouldn't betray her.

"You don't know me now," he pointed out. And neither did he, really.

"After last night, I think we know each other pretty well," she said.

Heat flashed through him with his desire for her. He wanted her again. No matter how many times he'd had her the night before, he had to have her again.

He shoved his hands into his pockets, resisting the urge to drag her up against him, to hold her close and kiss her like he needed to kiss her. Instead, he focused on the emotions he'd experienced at the hospital and asked, "How well do you know Vonner?"

"Agent Vonner?"

He nodded. He'd felt the man in the waiting room, felt the anger and frustration rolling off him. Though weaker, it had been eerily similar to the killer's emotions that Trent had felt at the crime scene. "Yeah, how well do you know him?"

She shrugged. "He only got assigned to the case with me a few months ago. I don't really know much about him."

"Why not?" he asked.

"Because I'm not interested," she said.

"Maybe you should be."

Her eyes widened with surprise. "What? You think he and I would make a good couple?"

Jealousy and possessiveness tightened the muscles in his stomach and had him clenching his jaw. Her lips curved into a smile, and he knew that she was still attuned to his emotions. That she felt what he felt…

But right now it was Vonner's emotions that concerned him. He remarked, "I think I would suspect the motives of anyone who wanted to get close to this case."

Her eyes widened in surprise. "How did you know he requested the assignment?"

"I didn't know that for certain, until now," he said with a wink.

She reached out, as if to smack him, but pulled her hand back before she touched him. He obviously wasn't the only one who didn't trust himself.

He continued. "Why would a guy like him, young and ambitious, want to be assigned to a cold case?"

Her blond brows drew together. "I didn't think about that."

"Maybe because he knew it wouldn't stay cold for long?"

She sucked in a breath. "I hadn't considered…"

"Vonner as a suspect?" he finished for her. "No, you were too busy considering me."

"Another thought occurred to me," she said. "Another suspect."

"Who?" he asked.

Again self-disgust filled him for having passed out. What if the killer had been there? Sure, there had been uniforms guarding the perimeter of the crime scene. But if the killer could be Vonner, it could have been one of those men, too. Trent had left her alone and vulnerable. Even though she could take care of herself, she'd been distracted by having to take care of him.

"Who's your new suspect?" he asked.

"The real killer."

"What do you mean?" He should have been

relieved she no longer suspected him, but he wasn't as easily convinced of his innocence.

"Until I met you, I figured he was still alive," she shared.

"Then you met me and you had a new suspect."

"But I think my first notion, my first instinct, was right," she said. "I think he's still alive. I don't think he died like his victims and like the detective died."

"We have no proof that Kooiyer is dead, either," he reminded her. No proof that Trent had been the lawman instead of the lunatic.

"No, we don't. We need more information." She stared at him, her gaze narrowed and pointed.

He had been working that morning, but he wouldn't share any more of what he'd written with her until he knew how it ended. Instead, he gestured toward the door to the morgue. "Isn't that why we're here?"

"You should wait for me in the hall," she insisted. "You don't have to go inside. You don't have to go through all that again." She stopped for a moment, then asked him, "What exactly did you feel back there? Did you feel him?"

He nodded. "Rage, hatred, madness…"

"What you'd expect from a sadistic killer." She reached out and squeezed his arm. "I'm sorry you had to experience that. But you don't have to feel this…what she went through."

"I don't have to," he agreed. "But I need to. We need to get this over." He would like to be as certain as she was that he hadn't been the killer thirty years ago. But while she could feel his emotions, she couldn't see the images he saw—the memories that had to have been his. So if he had been the one who'd started it all, it was appropriate that he would be the one to end it.

Alaina glanced from the mutilated body to Trent. Like at the apartment, she couldn't feel these emotions of his. Because they weren't his.

She could see them, though, on his handsome face as the color drained from it, leaving only the dark circles beneath his deep-set eyes.

"How'd she die?" she asked.

Dr. Rosenthal shook his head. "I haven't had a chance to do much more than look at her."

"I was asking him," she said, turning again to Trent even though she hated putting him through this again.

"It was more violent than last time."

"She has defensive wounds," the doctor said, lifting the victim's hand with its shredded nails.

"But he choked then stabbed her," Trent continued, his voice rough, "just like the other woman."

"Penelope Otten." As she said the name, something tugged at her memory. A screen name. PennyForYourThoughts. Could she have been…? "And this woman is Cordelia Stehouwer." She searched her mind again, trying to find a connection.

"They really have nothing in common," she mused aloud. "Penelope was a redhead, like those women who were murdered thirty years ago. But Cordelia is a blonde."

"Like you," Trent said.

Alaina shivered as his fear for her safety rushed over her. She opened her jacket, reminding him that she carried a gun. As hard as Cordelia had fought, Alaina could and would fight harder if she actually became the target of the killer.

"He didn't stab her when she was passed out," Trent said, his voice thick with horror. "He waited until she regained consciousness…"

Like the killer had with the other victim, and like the killer had in all Trent's books. Alaina flinched as she remembered the scene she'd just read. But it hadn't been just a scene in a book; it had been her murder.

The doctor, studying the skin around the jagged wound in the victim's chest, remarked, "I see something they had in common."

"Yeah, they're both missing their hearts," Alaina said, anger and frustration coursing through her. Trent's and hers.

"No, it's the skin around the wound," Dr. Rosenthal said. "There was an old scar. They both had old scars over their hearts. I can't understand what they're from. I thought maybe transplants, but I checked the first victim for transplant meds. She had nothing in her system. But then the scar looked old. It was so faint I nearly missed it."

Delray. That was what Cordelia had called herself online, on the website that Alaina had anonymously launched a couple of years ago and on which other women had anonymously posted. That must have been how the killer had chosen them. He had found the website Alaina had created, and he had done what she'd been unable to do. He'd tracked down the anonymous posters and made them his newest victims. But they weren't new victims; he'd already killed them once.

Just like in her previous life, these murders were her fault. These women were dead because of her, because of the mistake she'd made.

If not for the uniformed officers guarding the crime scene, he could have taken her there... where he'd already killed once. He could have taken her like he had before, right out from under her lover.

The man was weak. Why couldn't she see that she'd chosen the wrong lover? Why didn't she realize that she needed a real man in her life? One who would not neglect her as she'd been neglected before.

He wouldn't neglect her. He was just getting

ready for her. He had to kill the other women first. It was their destiny to die again, like they had before.

Just like she was his destiny...

## Chapter 13

"Where's Agent Paulsen?" the director asked as he settled into the chair behind his desk.

Not where Trent wanted her. Not back at his estate, locked away in his fortress so that the killer could not get to her. Frustration gnawed at Trent's control. He didn't need to be here, but he had been summoned. He would have ignored the summons if not for wanting some answers himself.

"She's still not feeling well," Trent said. And now it was no lie. She had gotten physically sick at the morgue, sick with guilt. It clutched at him also.

Those poor women...

"So she's really sick?" Graves asked, a gray brow lifted in skepticism. Behind the man stretched the bright lights of the city—and the people in that city whose emotions pummeled Trent.

Behind Trent only a glass wall separated him from the rest of the Bureau. Only one man's emotions pummeled him from there with nearly the same violence with which Vonner wanted to physically pummel him.

Tension pounded at Trent's temples and the base of his neck. "Yes, Agent Paulsen is sick, but she's still working the case."

Trent knew it, even though he had told her to stay put and wait for him and to keep her apartment door locked and open it only to him. Hell, he'd suggested that maybe she shouldn't even open it to him.

"What about you?"

"I'm here," Trent pointed out as he paced the spacious office, his concern for Alaina's safety making him anxious. He stopped before the director's granite-and-glass desk and asked, "Why did you ask me to come?"

"I wanted to talk to you," Graves said, his dark eyes glinting with amusement. "I granted you access for this case, so I could get a fresh perspective."

"That's why?" Trent asked. "I wondered why you gave me access."

"You and everyone else," the director said with a short laugh. "Agent Vonner thinks I'm crazy."

"Are you?"

Instead of being offended, the older man laughed. "I don't know what to think about any of this," Graves admitted. "It was supposed to be a cold case." His dark eyes narrowed as he studied Trent's face. "But it didn't stay a cold case."

"Do you think that's because of my books?" he asked, although he didn't really need confirmation.

Graves nodded. "Probably. You gave someone the horrific idea."

Trent sighed as the guilt pressed more heavily on his chest. "Yeah, I think so, too."

"So I'm curious about those books," Graves said.

"You said you were a fan." Which had surprised Trent because so few people in law enforcement enjoyed the horror series.

The director laughed again, but his dark eyes remained cold with suspicion. "I wouldn't go that far."

"Then I don't understand..." Trent dropped into a sling-back leather chair in front of the man's desk. "Why give me access?"

"Maybe I *am* crazy," Graves allowed, "or maybe my curiosity's getting the better of me."

"What makes you so curious about my books?" Trent wondered aloud.

"I was there thirty years ago," Graves admitted. "I was on the case back then."

"With the detective?"

He nodded. "I was the liaison between the local police department and the Bureau. I was there," he repeated, his voice echoing the frustration he must have felt during the serial killer's first reign of terror, "and I don't know some of the stuff you know, that you wrote about in your series of books. So, yeah, I'm curious. How do you know so many details about what happened? Who's your informant?"

"My informant?"

"Someone had to give you all those details. Is it Detective Kooiyer? Or the reporter... I can't remember his name." Graves leaned back in his chair and steepled his fingers over his protruding belly. "Hell, I guess it could have been Dr. Rosenthal."

"Dr. Rosenthal?" Trent thought of the Bureau coroner he and Alaina had left a short time ago, before Trent had driven her back to her apartment and made certain she locked herself inside.

"Rosenthal was with the city morgue back then," Graves remembered, "doing his internship. I'm sure it's a case he never forgot."

Trent's head pounded as he pondered all the suspects he had never considered before. Because he'd been convinced he was the killer.

But what if Alaina was right and the killer was still alive, still living his murderous life? Then who had Trent been that he remembered so many details of the murders?

"What about Detective Kooiyer?" he asked. Even though he had no respect for the man, he kind of hoped Alaina was right. "Have you kept in touch with him?"

Graves rubbed a hand over his face. "Kept in touch? I've kept looking for him."

"You don't know where he is?"

"No one knows," the director said, then narrowed those dark eyes with suspicion, "except maybe you."

Trent shook his head. "I've never met him. Tell me about him."

"He disappeared—" Graves shook his head in disgust "—both him and his wife, which was the craziest thing."

"You think they just ran off together," Trent asked, "or that something happened to them?"

Graves sighed. "I'd like to think that something happened to them."

Trent nearly gasped his surprise at the director's callous admission.

"I prefer it to the alternative," Graves explained, "that they deserted their young son. Then they wouldn't have been the people I thought they were."

An image flashed through Trent's mind of a giggling toddler being lifted high in his arms. The boy's pudgy face creased with a big smile, his brown eyes bright with joy, as he stared down at him. Of course, that didn't mean the child had been his son. If he'd been the killer, as the detective's friend, he could have been a doting uncle. "What happened to their son?"

The older man shrugged. "Some family must have taken him in. I don't remember."

And he obviously didn't care. But Trent cared. And so would Alaina—if he told her. But first he had to get back to her, had to make sure she was safe. Then he would decide if she could handle any more guilt; she already blamed herself for too much of what had happened then and was happening again.

Trent glanced at his watch. "So why'd you call me here tonight?"

"Vonner wants to bring you in for questioning."

"Is that what this is?" he asked. "An interview?"

Graves laughed. "I asked my questions, but you never really answered them."

"I don't have any answers for you," Trent admitted. "But when I do, you'll know."

Graves nodded and waved a hand, dismissing him.

Finally.

\* \* \*

"So you decided to open the door to me," Trent said as he stepped inside her apartment.

Alaina lifted the gun from behind her back and showed him that she'd been prepared to defend herself. "Make you feel better?"

He grinned. "Yeah. I have to remind myself that you can take care of yourself."

"Of myself? Yes." She sighed, the guilt overwhelming. "But I haven't done a good job of taking care of other people." She should have known that if his victims could find one another in this life, the killer could find them, too. And she'd made it a hell of a lot easier for him with her website.

"Is this it?" he asked as he stared at the laptop she'd left open on the breakfast bar. He leaned over and studied the screen. "Déjà Vu?"

"Yeah. I started the website so that I could find other people like me, people with memories of another life." So that she hadn't felt so alone and like such a freak.

"I didn't know about this," he said.

"You wouldn't have looked for it. You denied that your memories were really memories, probably like most people do." Except for those women who had posted on her site and had admitted to having unexplained scars, too. But they, like her, had remained anonymous, in order to protect themselves from more rejection or prejudice. How had he found them?

"You posted a warning," Trent said as he read the flashing banner.

She shivered, knowing that it wasn't enough.

He read it aloud. "'Two members of this site have been recent victims of the same murders that claimed their past lives. Take precautions.'"

"Maybe I should have had you write it," she admitted. "It would have made more sense."

"I don't know how else you could have said it. You got your point across." But then he read the rest and turned back to her, his green eyes filled with concern. "You want them to contact you if they feel they're in danger or if they suspect anyone of following them? Alaina, you're going to lead the killer right to you."

"It might be the only way to protect the other women who are still out there."

"What about you? Who'll protect you?" he demanded.

"I can protect myself," she reminded him. "I only wish…"

Her guilt and frustration struck Trent. "It's not your fault," he assured her. "It's not your fault. And now you're doing everything you can to protect them, including putting yourself in danger."

"It's too late. Too little…" Her voice cracked with the tears she'd been fighting. "And it is all my fault."

He pulled her into his arms. As ever, passion flared between them, but he offered her comfort instead. He just held her as she cried, her fists clutching his shirt.

Trent intended to share with her the information he'd learned from the director, at least some of it. He wasn't sure he could tell her about her son and not destroy her. But he couldn't tell her anything he'd learned about potential suspects for the old murders, either, not right now. She couldn't handle thinking any more about the murders tonight. She shouldn't be thinking at all, because all that chased through her mind was guilt and regret.

As he'd been able to earlier, at his house, he

could read her emotions now. The connection between them was so strong, so unbreakable.

She lifted her face to his gaze. Even with her skin blotchy with tears, her eyes red, she was still the most beautiful woman he'd ever known. He wiped away the last traces of moisture with the pads of his thumbs.

"You are in danger, too," he reminded her. "You need to be careful. It could be anyone."

"It's not you," she insisted. "I won't believe that it's you."

"I don't know who I was," he warned her again. "But I know who you were."

"A tramp," she said.

He shook his head. "Everything. You were everything to me, and I think you are again. I can't lose you."

"You won't," she assured him, offering him comfort when she needed it so much herself. "You won't lose me...."

Trent didn't just think it anymore; he knew. He loved her.

Her eyes widened with surprise, as if she felt it. He wouldn't give her the words yet, not with a killer after her and another killer potentially inside him. But he could show her how much she meant to him.

He leaned down and pressed his lips to her swollen eyelids in a tender kiss. Her breath shuddered out soft and warm against his throat. Then her mouth pressed against his neck, to where his pulse throbbed with excitement at her closeness.

Her fingers grasped his T-shirt, then dragged it up his torso and over his head. She ran her hands over his hair, smoothing the strands she'd disheveled. Then she touched his shoulders, arms and chest, her palms warm against his skin. "Trent…"

"Shh…" he murmured against her lips, brushing his mouth across hers. She parted her lips and the tip of her tongue darted out to touch his. He slid his tongue across her bottom lip, in and out of her mouth.

She moaned, her neck arching. Then she pulled back and urged him, "Take me to bed."

His body shuddered with the overwhelming need to connect with her physically as well as emotionally. But he pulled back, reining in his tenuous control. "Alaina, you're exhausted."

She shook her head. "I will always want you," she insisted, "even when I'm dead."

He shuddered again, with foreboding over her declaration. Even when she was dead…?

Earlier she had denied the danger he knew she was in, but she must have accepted that it was true. Imminent even…

"Trent…" She wrapped her arms around his shoulders, then lifted her legs and wrapped them around his waist. "Take me to bed."

He clutched her butt and walked in the direction she pointed, toward the door of a short hall. As they moved, her hips ground against his erection, hardening his body to the point of pain.

Pain only she could relieve.

A lamp beside the bed illuminated her room with a soft glow. The pale yellow sheets echoed the pale yellow walls and the drapes pulled back at the window. Everything light and bright despite—or maybe because of—all the darkness she'd seen in her mind and in her new life as a federal agent.

She unhooked her legs and slid down his body, her chest tight against his bare one, her hips arching against his erection. "I imagined you here with me after you left that night," she admitted. "But I thought the scar turned you off."

He shook his head. "You're beautiful…" He lifted her sweater, pulled it over her head and tossed it aside. Then he reached for her, his fingers shaking slightly as he ran the tip of one along the faint white ridge. "This overwhelms me," he admitted, "with everything it represents, everything it proves true."

"I still could be one of those other women," she remarked, almost desperately. "One of those women who'd been unfortunate enough to have the wrong coloring."

"You know you're not," he gently reminded her. "Because of this…because of us…"

And the passion that burned between them with an otherworldly intensity.

Her breath shuddered out as his fingers continued to stroke her scar. Then he unclasped her bra and pushed the straps from her shoulders. The bra fell away from her breasts as it dropped to the floor.

His hands along her sides, he pulled her close,

so that her nipples, peaked with her desire, rubbed against his chest. And he lowered his mouth to hers, kissing her like he always kissed her, as if he'd die without her lips, her breath. If anything happened to her...

He clutched her closer to him, consuming her with his mouth and his tongue. Alaina's nails raked down his back as she arched against him. She moaned deep in her throat, sending her need and her heat rushing through him, burning him up.

His hands shaking now, he caught her waist and pulled her back, just long enough to unclasp her pants and shove them and her lace panties over her hips and down her long legs. Then he dealt with the rest of his clothes and pulled a condom from his wallet.

Alaina took it from his fingers and tore open the foil. Then she closed her hands around his erection, sliding her palm up and down the pulsing length of him.

He closed his eyes on a wave of sensation. Her desire and his filled his heart, tensing every muscle in his body so that he was taut and on the edge of control. He expected the latex of the condom to replace her fingers, so he jerked when instead he felt the wet heat of her mouth as her lips closed over the tip of his penis.

He opened his eyes and stared down at where she'd dropped to her knees before him. Her eyes dark with passion, she stared up at him, watching his face as she loved him with her mouth. Her tongue slid along his erection as she sucked him deep in her throat.

"Alaina," he warned her as she pushed him dangerously close to the edge of no control. His fingers clutched the silky strands of her hair, holding her head against him. But it wasn't enough. He had to completely connect his body with hers. His soul with hers… "No."

She pulled back, those gray-blue eyes glittering with power and passion. Then she rolled the condom over the length of his erection.

He nearly came then, the tension wound so tight inside him that it might only take her briefest touch. But that wouldn't have been fair to her.

She needed this, needed him. He felt it. He felt everything she felt. And the sensations were heady.

He reached out, flicking first his thumbs over her nipples. Her eyes dilated, and her breath caught. And he felt the quiver in her stomach, the heat between her legs. So he moved one hand there, to slip his fingers inside her as he lowered his mouth to her breasts and began loving them with his tongue and his lips.

Her legs trembled, and she tightened her thighs around his hand, the soft skin of her inner thighs brushing against his palm. Passion, hot and wet, poured over his fingers as she came, her orgasm spilling out of her with a throaty moan.

And his control snapped. He pushed her back against the mattress, then he followed her down and pushed her legs apart. She lifted them high around his back, her nails digging into his butt as she guided his erection inside her. She screamed, coming again with just that first thrust. But he wasn't done. He needed the friction, the in and out, her inner muscles tightening around him like a fist in a velvet glove, stroking him, holding him....

She came again, her eyes wide with shock as her body shuddered. He pushed her, thrusting harder, faster, until he joined her in oblivion, his orgasm shaking him to the core with its intensity.

Overwhelmed, he nearly gave her the words, nearly professed his love. But then she might feel she needed to reciprocate, and he couldn't accept her love. Because she couldn't love a man neither of them really knew....

Rage bubbled over as he read the message she'd posted. She thought she could stop him? His hands gripped the laptop, then hurled it against the wall. It dented the drywall, then cracked and dropped to the floor, pieces of plastic snapping off. Like his temper.

She was with *him*. Again. He should kill them both now. Set a fire…

Or break down the door and steal both their hearts.

## Chapter 14

"Are you feeling better, Agent Paulsen?"

No. But she nodded in response to the director's question. She should have come to the Bureau with Trent when he'd met with Graves the night before, but then Alaina had had something more important to do. She'd had to try to correct the mistake she had made, the mistake that had already cost two women their lives.

Trent had wanted to come with her this morning. He'd insisted on it, but she'd convinced him she'd be fine at the Bureau. She hadn't been as certain that he would be, with Vonner considering him the prime suspect in the recent murders.

"I'm sorry to have been out when I was needed," she told her superior.

"Baines told me that you were still working the case," Graves said. "And the calls we've been getting confirm that you have."

"Calls?" Her breath caught as fear and hope gripped her. Maybe some of the women had seen something or suspected someone? They would finally have a lead on the Thief of Hearts. But what would that lead cost? The safety of innocent women? "You've been receiving calls?"

"Yes, from some *website* you set up." The disdain in his voice left no doubt as to his opinion on reincarnation.

After her own father's rejection, she wasn't surprised by his reaction. She could have pulled aside the cowl neck of her sweater and shown him the scar. But even with Dr. Rosenthal's discovery of those same scars on the murder victims, she doubted the director would change his mind about a philosophy so many struggled to understand or accept.

"Apparently you offered federal protection to

these women," Graves continued, and now the disdain had turned to disapproval.

The women had requested protection? Goose bumps rose along the skin on Alaina's arms despite the jacket she wore over her sweater. "Yes, sir."

"Who authorized you to offer federal protection to anyone, Agent Paulsen?" he demanded to know, his deep voice vibrating with anger.

"I—I…hadn't thought I would need authorization," she explained. "These women are in danger."

"We have no proof of that."

"Two women have been brutally murdered," Alaina said, stunned and disappointed that she had to remind him.

"We have no proof that those murders are linked to this website or to past lives." He grimaced now with his obvious opinion of reincarnation. "And if I had been made aware of this website you created, you never would have been assigned to this case."

"I'm sorry, sir. I may have overstepped," she said, though she didn't understand how, when lives were at risk. "But I honestly believe these women are in danger. Dr. Rosenthal found scars on the two recent victims—"

Director Graves lifted a hand, as if to forestall her argument. "You've put the Bureau and me in an untenable position, Agent Paulsen."

Confusion knitted her brows together while tension pounded at her temples. She didn't need this lecture; she needed to be working the leads from those phone calls. "Untenable? I don't understand."

A muscle ticked along his clenched jaw. "If the media gets wind of this, it would be an embarrassment to the Bureau."

"Embarrassment?" Her voice cracked as anger rushed through her. "Isn't it more of an embarrassment that a killer who eluded the Bureau for thirty years is killing again?" She snorted. "Embarrassment? Hell, it's a travesty that this case was ever allowed to become cold."

The director slammed his fist onto his desk. "There were no leads!"

Apparently Graves was as familiar with those cold-case files as Alaina was. "Maybe if someone had kept working it, there would have been leads. Some more evidence could have turned up. Something…"

"You think this is the same killer—the one from thirty years ago?" He uttered a derisive laugh. "You think someone who killed, like he killed, would have been able to stop for thirty years?"

"Some do. They have to," she reminded him. "They get caught, or put away for some reason." Or they'd killed the person who had inspired their killing and they didn't need to kill again until they realized she'd returned to life—thanks to her ill-conceived website.

She would like to think that she'd started Déjà Vu to find answers. But she'd started the site because she'd needed validation. She had needed to prove to herself that she wasn't crazy for having those memories of another life. That she wasn't alone…

And maybe she'd hoped to find that man who'd haunted her dreams, waking and asleep.

Graves offered an alternative. "Or the old killer died, and someone's books detailing those murders has inspired someone to copy those crimes." His dark eyes narrowed as he stared at her. "You're his source."

"What?"

"Your boyfriend—Baines—how long have you known him?" the director imperiously asked. "Since he started writing that first book back in college? Had you and he tracked down the old newspaper articles?"

"Articles?"

"There was a reporter who followed the case," he shared. "He was close to the detective."

"How do you know this?" she asked. There had been no mention of a reporter in those files. Of course, even now law enforcement wouldn't admit to a relationship with someone from the media.

Graves answered her question with one of his own. "How do you know Baines?"

"I just met him a few days ago," she insisted. In this life. In another she had known him for a long time, and she had known him well.

The director snorted his disbelief. "Agent Vonner is working the connection between you two. He's going to find it."

"Agent Vonner is wasting his time when he

should be tracking down the leads from those calls."

"Those calls are a nuisance we don't need right now." He leaned back in his chair, his gaze cold as he stared at her. "But they have helped me realize what I need to do."

She shivered, knowing this was not going to be good for her...or Trent.

The guy sighed regretfully, but his eyes were cold and determined. "I have to let you go."

"Let me go? What do you mean?"

"You're fired," he explained. "Turn in your gun and your shield, and a guard will escort you out of the building."

"Director—"

"If you want to petition to keep your job, I recommend that you hire a lawyer, Ms. Paulsen." Graves thumped his hand against his desk. "You might want to tell your boyfriend to do the same."

"Vonner convinced you he's a viable suspect," she realized.

The director nodded. "He's the only suspect who makes sense. To write what he has, he's sick. Twisted. Eventually he'd grow tired of just writing about these crimes—he'd be tempted to actually commit one. Now two…"

"You're wrong about him. Vonner's wrong about him," she insisted, more outraged at their maligning of Trent's character than her firing.

Graves shook his head. "I used to think that you were so smart, Ms. Paulsen. But you're making mistakes, mistakes that will probably, at best, get you arrested. At worst, get you killed."

"I can take care of myself," she assured him. Her hand shaking, Alaina laid her gun and credentials on the cold granite surface of the director's desk. "I want to know if you'll protect those women."

"That's no longer any of your concern," he callously reminded her.

"Yes, it is," she insisted, anger and frustration gripping her. "I promised them protection."

"You didn't have the authority to do that, Ms. Paulsen," he reprimanded her again. "Now I must order you to leave the premises."

"Sir, you have to—"

The older man stood and slammed his fists onto the desk next to her gun and shield. "Leave now, Ms. Paulsen, or I'll have you arrested for interfering with an ongoing investigation."

She bit her lip to resist the temptation to continue arguing. If she got arrested, she wouldn't be able to help those women at all. She turned and headed for the door, but before she closed it behind her, she couldn't resist adding, "You're going to regret this...."

"This is crazy," Trent said, outrage heating his skin so that his face burned beneath the stubble on his jaw. "Let me talk to him. I think I can get through to him, convince him to give you your job back."

"Or you'll get arrested like he threatened to arrest me," Alaina warned him. She leaned her head against the headrest of the rental car and closed her eyes. "You're their number-one suspect right now."

He sighed. "That actually makes sense. If I were them, I'd suspect me, too."

"And they suspect I'm either your accomplice or your unwitting dupe."

"What?" Outrage on her behalf surged through him again. How could anyone suspect her involvement in a murder? "No wonder they can't find the real killer."

"Vonner's working on finding a connection between us."

He laughed. "I doubt it's a connection he'll be able to understand, let alone accept." His amusement faded. Trent wasn't certain it was a connection *he* could accept.

"They think I've been your source all along."

Frustration tightened the muscles in his neck and shoulders. He shrugged. "They're fools. We need to go back in there and set them straight. You can show them the scar...."

"No." She shook her head. "I think it's better we stay away from the Bureau right now." She opened her eyes, turned in the passenger seat and studied him where he sat behind the wheel of the rental car. "Thanks to you, we already know more than anyone in the Bureau does."

"I'm not so sure about that," he said. "The director was on the case, you know. He worked it thirty years ago with Detective Kooiyer."

A breath hissed out between Alaina's clenched

teeth. "He's late fifties, early sixties," she mused. "He could have been the detective's friend."

"Could have been," Trent admitted.

Alaina pressed her hand to her heart. "Which puts those women even more at risk. No wonder he's refused to offer them protection."

Trent cursed. This was why he preferred to lock himself away from the real world. It was easier to not get involved than to care too much— like Alaina cared. He could feel her frustration and pain as if it were his own. He reached across the console for her hand, but she pulled away and opened the glove box.

He noticed how sunlight glinted off metal and looked down to see a handgun. "You had a gun in there?"

She nodded. "I didn't know what might happen today. I didn't know what Vonner had been telling Graves."

"So you think Vonner's the reason you got fired?"

She lifted her slender shoulders in a slight shrug. "I don't know. He's focused more on you than me."

"You rejected him," he reminded her. "He

might have gone after you out of spite." The hair lifted on Trent's nape as his instincts screamed at him. "I wonder just how obsessed with you he is…."

As obsessed as the Thief of Hearts?

"I'm more concerned about those other women with the scars," Alaina said as she inspected the clip for the gun. "I promised them protection. I need to make sure they're safe."

"I figured you might say that." He knew her so well, felt all her guilt and pain. "So I put my techie guy on it and got some IP addresses."

Her eyes widened in surprise. "So did he find out who anyone is?"

He nodded. "As he claims, no one's really anonymous online."

"Did he find any of their actual home addresses?" she asked, hope pitching her voice higher.

He nodded again. "A couple more women live right here in the city."

"I've heard that reincarnated people are drawn back to the same places where they lived in other lives." She stared at him, her pupils dilating with desire. "And to the same people they loved in other lives."

He wanted to give her the words; she deserved the words. But until he knew for certain which man he'd been to her—husband or killer—he could not offer her anything. Nothing but an uncertain future…after a painful, terrifying past.

"Trent?" she called his name, her voice soft with a vulnerability he suspected she rarely ever showed.

He clenched his fingers around the steering wheel, resisting the urge to reach for her, to drag her across the console and into his arms. He had no idea who could be watching them—Director Graves, Agent Vonner or the killer.

"I, uh, my briefcase's in the back," he said. "The list of addresses is on the top."

Disappointment dimmed the brightness of her gray-blue eyes, but she reached between the front seats and pulled the steel briefcase from the back. She whistled as she opened it. "I'm not the only one who's armed," she observed as she touched the handle of his Glock.

"I'm not going to let anything happen to you."

He hadn't protected her in their past life; he wouldn't make that same mistake.

"I can protect myself," she said again, her voice sharp with pride. "It's these women I'm worried about." She read an address from the list. "This one's nearby. Just a few blocks from here."

Fighting the congestion of rush-hour traffic, Trent followed her directions. Her voice cracked with urgency as she called out the streets and which direction he was to turn on them. She leaned forward, her breasts pushing against the seat belt, her fingers tapping on the dash.

Her anxiety and dread filled him. But he resisted the urge to reach for her hand, to offer her comfort. His touch wouldn't be enough to ease her fears. Only finding these women alive and safe would ease her worry.

But the closer they drew to the address, the more emotions overwhelmed him. The fear and panic. And the rage and hatred. His hand shook as he shut off the car.

Her breath caught, her eyes widening as she studied his face. "Trent…?"

"He's here," he warned Alaina. "The killer is still here."

# Chapter 15

"Stay here," Alaina whispered to Trent as if the killer could hear them out in the drive, in the car with the windows rolled up. Her heart beat louder than her voice, as it pounded fast and hard with fear and adrenaline when she reached for the door handle.

"Hell, no," he protested. "You're not going in there alone." He pulled his gun from the metal briefcase and pushed open his door the same time she opened hers.

The creak of metal hinges echoed loudly in the eerie quiet of the suburban street. The houses, some with porch lights left on, looked empty, as if everyone had already left for work or school.

She glanced back at Trent and wanted to argue with him, but there wasn't time—not if the killer had already found his next victim. Thanks to her unwitting help.

"Stay behind me," she snapped at him as she headed toward the front door of the small bungalow. The door, which had been painted a startlingly bright yellow, stood ajar.

Alaina tightened her grip on the gun. "Be careful," she whispered to Trent before ducking inside the foyer. She had no doubt he would follow her inside. She felt his fear and adrenaline as acutely as she felt her own.

But that wasn't all Trent felt. She glanced behind her and noted the paleness of his skin, the tightness of his jaw and the horror in his eyes. And she knew what she would find even before she pushed open the bedroom door to the blood sprayed across the wall.

She rushed toward the bed on which the woman lay and checked for a pulse. But there was no need to do so; the victim's empty chest gaped open. "That son of a bitch!"

A crash reverberated down the hall from somewhere in the house. Trent rushed out ahead of her, the gun she didn't even know if he could fire clenched in his hand. His legs longer, he beat her out the back door, which swung out on the porch in the wake of someone else having just passed through it. But she saw nothing but a shadow among the trees of the backyard.

Trent lifted his gun, but she grabbed his shoulder. "No, you can't shoot. You can't know for sure if that's him." And not another innocent person caught in the cross fire of an obsession that spanned lifetimes.

"I know. I can feel that it's him," Trent insisted. Yet he lowered his weapon and a ragged sigh slipped through his lips. "We were too late."

He'd stayed behind her, in the hall; he hadn't seen what she had on the bed. But he must have felt it—all that poor woman's terror and pain...

"Yes, we were too late," she confirmed. Tears of frustration and guilt burned her eyes. How had she been so careless, so stupid? Again?

"This isn't your fault," he tried to reassure her.

But Alaina knew better.

"We need to call this in," she said as they stepped back inside the house.

"No need," Vonner said, his gun trained on them. "I'm already here. And you're both under arrest."

"So you've decided to live out the books you write," Vonner taunted Trent.

Trent bit the inside of his cheek to hold in a pithy response. He wouldn't give the smug agent the satisfaction of goading him into talking. Instead, he leaned back as far as the stiff chair would allow, pushing away from the table to which one of his wrists was cuffed. The metal was cold and hard against his skin. He studied the mirror across from him; it was the only thing that relieved the monotony of the gray cement walls and floor of the interrogation room at the Bureau.

"You fooled Alaina," the agent continued. "But I understand how you managed that now, after seeing that website. She's not exactly stable herself."

Under the table Trent clenched his hands into fists that he longed to slam into Vonner's face. Again and again. But he wasn't feeling only his own rage. He felt Vonner's, as well. His anger and resentment.

"You probably believe in that reincarnation crap, too," Vonner continued. "Or is her belief just convenient for you? Did you use it to get her into bed?"

"Wouldn't you like to know?" Trent shot back, unable to hold down the words.

"So you and she do have a sexual relationship? Did you kill that woman together today?" he asked. "Is murder foreplay for you two?"

"You are one sick bastard," Trent said, disgust choking him. "And you're not too smart."

Vonner snorted, not really insulted by Trent's opinion of his intelligence.

"I already asked for my lawyer," he reminded the overzealous agent. "Anything you get out of me now would be inadmissible in court."

"So you do have something to hide," Vonner persisted, pouncing on everything Trent said like a cat chasing a piece of string. Or its own tail...

"Don't we all?" Trent shot back, wondering what the agent had to hide. And while he shouldn't answer any questions until his lawyer showed up, he could ask some. So he voiced the question that had been burning his throat since Vonner had showed up at the murder scene. "Did you follow us when we left the Bureau this morning?"

Or had he beat them there? Had he been the shadow that Trent should have shot at through the trees? Vonner could have killed the woman, slipped out the back and then around to the front to arrest them.

The agent said nothing, but his jaw clenched so tightly a muscle ticked in his cheek.

"If you followed us, you know we had no time to kill her," Trent pointed out. But if he'd followed them, Vonner couldn't be the killer, either, unless he'd killed her earlier and someone else had gone out the back door. Some unsuspecting witness…

But the only fear Trent had felt at the scene had been the residual of the dead woman's terror. And the only guilt had been Alaina's.

"I didn't follow you," Vonner admitted, putting himself right back at the top of Trent's suspect list.

"Then how'd you show up when you did?"

Vonner chuckled. "Yeah, that was kind of inconvenient for you."

"We were going to call it in." Trent reminded him of what Alaina had said.

"Sure."

"So tell me," Trent urged him, "how you happened to be there."

"The woman called in earlier," Vonner explained, "to request protection. She claimed to have noticed someone watching her house. I suspected that someone was you. I was bringing your picture to show her."

His dark eyes narrowed. "Of course, it's hard to find a good picture of you. The one on your book jacket has your hand over your face, as if you're trying to hide your identity."

He planted his palms on the metal table and leaned forward. "What are you trying to hide, Baines? That you're a killer?" Vonner leaned even closer and whispered, "Your secret's out."

"What's the secret that made you request the assignment to this cold case?" Trent asked the other question that had been niggling at him for some time concerning Alaina's partner. "What's your motive, Vonner?"

The man straightened up and stepped back to lean against the mirror behind him. "Motive?"

"Something's driving you." Trent could feel the man's determination; it went deeper than mere ambition. It felt more like an obsession. With the case or with Alaina? "What's your secret, Vonner?"

The agent laughed. "Besides the fact that your lawyer's actually been waiting for you? Nothing. I'm not hiding a damn thing. I'll tell you straight out that I think you're the guy. And I'm going to prove it."

Trent was almost tempted to encourage Vonner to prove what guy he was. But just as he was reluctant to write the ending of the final book in the *Thief of Hearts* series, he was reluctant to know for certain who he'd been. If he had been the man he feared he'd been, he would have to walk away from Alaina—to protect her from himself.

But right now she needed protection from someone else.

"The lawyer is going to represent Alaina, too. Where is she?"

"Waiting for you," Vonner admitted, shaking

his head with disgust. "I don't know why I never noticed it before."

"What?" curiosity compelled Trent to ask.

"How crazy she is…" Vonner pushed his hand through his dark hair and sighed his disappointment.

"She's not crazy," Trent insisted. "You can't tell me you've never had that sense of déjà vu, that conviction that you've been somewhere before, done something before. But it's not a memory from this life, so it must be a memory from another life."

Like those images Trent had had, images of making love with a woman who'd meant everything to him. But those images, and the feelings they'd inspired, paled in comparison to what he felt with Alaina.

Vonner shook his head. "Nope. Never."

Trent narrowed his eyes over how quickly the man had answered, his denial too vehement. Did some old memories haunt Vonner, too? Memories of him killing?

"How old are you?" he asked the agent.

"None of your damn business," Vonner shot back at him.

Trent studied the man's face. Few lines rimmed his dark eyes or his smirking mouth. He was young, probably around the same or close to Trent's age. He could have been less than thirty. He could have been the original Thief of Hearts.…

"You've really never remembered anything," Trent persisted, "that didn't happen in this life? That had to have happened in another life?"

Vonner shuddered, as if unnerved, either by Trent's questions or those memories he denied having. He jumped as knuckles rapped against the mirror behind him. Then he walked around to where Trent sat and unlocked the handcuff that tethered him to the table.

"I suspect I will have a déjà vu moment," the agent admitted, "when I get you back in that chair and finally get you to answer my questions."

"We can talk with my lawyer present," Trent offered, rubbing the chafed skin of his wrist. Vonner couldn't have made the cuff much tighter. "I have nothing to hide. I just don't trust you." Not with his legal rights and definitely not with Alaina's life.

Despite her pain over being fired, Trent was

actually relieved that she would no longer be working with this man. He suspected Vonner had no doubts about who he was and who he'd been, but he'd chosen to keep it secret.

"No. You're free to go…for now." The guy's dark eyes narrowed with hatred. A hatred that felt eerily familiar in intensity to what Trent had experienced at the last two murder scenes.

He stood, then swayed slightly on his feet, as the feeling overwhelmed him. And blackness rushed in, momentarily blinding him as it threatened his consciousness.

The agent cursed and grabbed his shoulder, his fingers biting in a fierce grasp. "You're not going to freakin' pass out again," Vonner ordered him. "Alaina might have fallen for your games, but I'm not as easily fooled."

Not like Detective Kooiyer had been fooled… by his wife, by his best friend. It was no wonder that so much disgust filled Trent when he'd written the detective's scenes. He'd thought it had been the killer's disdain.

Now he wondered…

If Vonner had once been the killer, then Trent

had to have been the detective. The only problem with that scenario, however, was that he could not believe they had ever been friends.

# Chapter 16

"Are you all right?" Trent asked Alaina as he closed and locked her apartment door behind them.

She nodded and lied. "Fine."

"You didn't talk to anyone without the lawyer?" he asked, his voice rough with concern.

"I did," she admitted, unrepentant over what she'd said. It was the only thing she didn't regret having done. "I made it clear that the director knew those women were in danger but refused to protect them. I made it clear that the woman's family will also be made aware of that.

Maybe they'll protect the other ones on that list. Obviously I can't…"

Her voice cracked, her heart aching with regret and pain. "I've screwed everything up, Trent. I'm trying to help but I just keep making everything worse."

He pulled her into his arms, his hands stroking her back as if trying to soothe her. "It's not your fault. You've done nothing wrong. I'm the one who started this all up again. I shouldn't have written those books."

She wasn't the only one struggling with guilt and regret. She wrapped her arms around his waist, clutching the soft cotton of his T-shirt, holding him as close as they could get with clothes between them.

"You didn't know," she reminded him, "that what you wrote was real."

"It doesn't matter if it was real or not," Trent said. "It gave someone the idea to make it real. This could just be someone copying those killings from the books. It may have nothing to do with the past."

"I doubt that," she said, "and so do you. He's going after those women from my website for a reason. Because he wants to kill them again. These murders aren't the work of some crazed fan of yours." She couldn't let Trent take the blame for what she had caused in this life and their past.

"Alaina…" His fingertips ran along her jaw, tipping her face up to his. "It's not your fault, either."

Tears stung her eyes and filled her throat. She could only shake her head.

"You're in more danger than those women." His fingertips slid down her throat, and his hands closed around her neck.

Her breath backed up in her lungs as fear choked her. Had she been wrong about him? Had she fallen for the killer?

But he pushed her chin up with his thumbs and lowered his head to hers. Just before his lips touched hers, she glimpsed a flash of pain and disappointment in the depths of his green eyes. And she felt it, just as he must have felt her fear.

"I'm sorry," she murmured against his lips.

He kissed her, softly, sweetly, his hands tangling in her hair. Then he pulled back and rested his forehead against hers. "Come home with me," he urged her. "Let me take you back to the estate. Let me keep you safe this time, Alaina."

She shook her head. "Not yet..."

"C'mon, you have nothing keeping you here," he insisted. "You got fired from your job."

"Those women are keeping me here. I have to make sure they're safe." She gestured toward the locked door. "I have to go back out there." There was one more woman on the list who lived in Detroit.

"After what you said, the director will offer them protection now," he assured her. "You've done all you can do without getting yourself killed. Please, let me get you out of here."

She glanced at the darkened window. "In the morning," she agreed, "and on one condition."

He arched a dark blond brow. "What?"

"That you write the rest..." She swallowed hard, choking on the emotion, the fear that rose up. "That you write the ending."

"Yeah." He pushed a hand through his hair and sighed. "It's time. It's time to end it."

She lifted her hand to his face, her fingers trembling. She knew what it meant. If he discovered that he had been the killer, he wouldn't trust himself around her. He would lock himself away in that fortress of his and never come out. Never touch her, never kiss her…

And if he'd been what he feared most, she shouldn't want him to. She shouldn't want anything to do with the man who had the soul of a serial killer.

"It can't be you," she said as she stroked his cheek. "It can't be you."

"Not now," he agreed. "There is someone else out there now, killing those women. I felt him today, at the house. I felt his rage, his hatred…" His throat moved as he swallowed hard. "And it felt familiar. So familiar. It could have been me in the past."

She shook her head, refusing to believe it. She moved her hands to his nape and pulled his mouth down to hers. He kissed her now with passion, all his conflicted emotions pouring over her. His fear, regret, desire…

He lifted her, his hands cupping her butt. She wrapped her legs around his waist, rubbing against the hard erection that strained against the fly of his jeans. A moan burned in her throat, spilling from her lips as Trent pulled his mouth from hers.

He lifted up her sweater, pulling it off and dropping it to the floor. Her bra followed.

Her legs still locked around his waist, Alaina dragged up his shirt and pulled it over his head. Then she skimmed her hands up and down his chest, his muscles rippling beneath her palms. He was so beautiful her breath caught with awe of his masculine perfection.

She leaned forward and pressed her lips to his shoulder. She had to taste him, so she slid her tongue across his salty-sweet skin. Then she nipped at him with her teeth.

"If you keep touching me like that, I won't make it to the bedroom," he warned her.

She shifted her hips, rubbing against him. Heat pooled between her legs, and a moan burned in her throat. "I don't want to wait, either."

Passion darkened his eyes as he met her gaze. He released her and jerked open the snap of her pants. Metal ground against metal as he dragged down the zipper, then pushed her slacks and her lace panties to the floor. Like her clothes, he dropped to his knees on the hardwood.

She reached out, grasping his shoulders, worried that once again his empathy had overwhelmed him. "Are you all right?"

"No," he said. "I have to taste you. Right now." He laid her back against the floor and slid her legs over his shoulders. The sinewy muscles rippled beneath the sensitive skin of her inner thighs.

She arched as his mouth found her. His tongue flicked across the throbbing center of her desire, and his hands slid up her body and cupped her breasts.

Her nipples pressed against his palms and she arched more, pressing harder. He moved his hands, so that his fingers touched the sensitive points. Between his thumb and forefinger, he squeezed them.

She bit her lip, but still a scream escaped. It grew louder as he pushed his tongue inside her. The pressure spiraled in intensity almost to the point of pain. She writhed against his mouth, trying to relieve it.

But Trent took his time, making love to her slowly with his mouth. Sliding his tongue in and out as his fingers teased her nipples. Finally

Alaina shattered, and tears spilled from the corners of her eyes, dripping into her hair as she arched her neck and screamed, her body shuddering in the throes of the orgasm.

His hands moved from her breasts. Then his zipper rasped. He didn't drop his jeans; he only freed his throbbing erection. Then he impaled her.

Veins stood out in a jagged zigzag at his temple. He grimaced, and she felt his pain. And hesitation.

"Condom," he murmured. "I need a condom."

"No," she assured him, wanting nothing between them anymore.

She wrapped her legs tight around his waist, holding him inside her. Then she leaned forward and pressed her mouth to his. She tasted her own passion on his lips, on his tongue as it slid inside her mouth, imitating the actions of his lower body as he thrust deeper inside her.

Her muscles stretched. She'd never felt him so deeply. Emotions like she'd never experienced overwhelmed her, intensifying the passion and the pressure that wound tight again inside her.

She clawed at his back, his butt, urging him to go faster.

He thrust harder and deeper, grunting and panting for breath as he chased his own desire. For her…

His feelings overwhelmed her. Then the release came over her, freeing her so that she felt weightless, as if she had escaped her own body. The orgasm shuddered through her, pleasure so extreme it curled her toes.

Then Trent stiffened, his body tense and anxious as he thrust one last time and came. His orgasm filled her. Somehow he still had the strength to carry her to the bedroom and collapse onto the mattress with her.

He rolled her against him, holding her tight in his arms, as if he never intended to let her go. His breath hot against her forehead, he murmured, "We should leave now."

She burrowed her face into the hollow between his neck and shoulder and pressed a kiss to his slick skin. "No. In the morning…"

She had something she needed to do before they left for the U.P., but she dare not tell him her plan. He would only try to talk her out of it.

## Chapter 17

Trent awoke alone in the dark. He didn't need to run his hands over the tangled sheets to know that Alaina had already left the bed. He didn't feel her.

And as he realized this, panic jerked him fully awake. Where the hell was she? Not close enough that he could feel her emotions, that he could know if she was afraid or angry or…

Even alive.

He hurried out of bed and first checked the window, pushing the curtains aside. The lock held, the glass unbroken. His heart pounding with fear and dread, he ran through the rest of the small apartment, checking first the door, which was locked, the jamb undisturbed. The living-room window was also locked and the glass unbroken.

No one had busted in and stolen her from him. She'd left of her own free will. Had she remembered something, some image that had scared her away?

He pushed his fingers through his hair. Panic had his heart beating fast and hard. "Alaina, where the hell are you?"

Knowing her, she had gone off to make sure those women were safe. Did she remember the addresses on the list? Or had she used her laptop, which he now noticed was missing, to contact the rest of the women?

Because he couldn't remember those addresses, Trent might have to contact the women through the blog, too. But would they trust someone they didn't know? After Alaina's warning regarding the murders, they shouldn't. How the hell was Trent going to find them—and Alaina?

When Vonner had searched his briefcase, the agent had taken what he'd called Trent's hit list.

Trent didn't know whether he did so in order to protect the women or to finish what he'd started.

Just thinking of Vonner brought forth emotions that overwhelmed Trent. The rage and hatred...

Did it come from the young agent...or the killer? Or were they, as Trent had begun to suspect, one and the same?

He had to know if the man was the reincarnated Thief of Hearts; he had to find Vonner before Vonner found Alaina.

She was in danger, and her life would be at risk until the killer was caught. For the first time Trent intended to use the very thing that had forced him to hide from civilization for the past decade.

He intended to use his empathy to find the killer.

"You can't stay here," Alaina warned the woman. "If he doesn't already know where you are, he soon will."

As grateful as she'd been to find Beverly Jachim alive, she worried that she couldn't keep her safe if the woman wouldn't listen to her.

Beverly, in her robe, cowered in a corner of her brightly flowered couch. Did she fear what might happen to her? Or did she just fear Alaina? "I have no place to go...."

"I know a place we can stay," Alaina said, thinking of Trent's estate, of his self-proclaimed fortress.

She'd promised to leave with him this morning. Now she noticed light streak across the sky as the sun began to rise. She doubted she would get back to the apartment before he awakened. He would be angry and hurt that she'd left him sleeping and snuck out. But she hadn't had the heart to wake him.

And she hadn't wanted to bring him along to what could have been another crime scene. She'd seen, and felt, how the residual emotions of the murders—from both the victim and the killer—overwhelmed him.

"We'll be safe there," she assured Beverly. "He won't be able to get to us." Trent would protect her or die trying; she didn't doubt that. She didn't doubt him, not like he doubted himself.

Beverly shook her head. "No. I shouldn't—I can't trust you...."

"Yes, you can," Alaina assured the other woman. "We've been talking for years online."

"About our memories, that scar…" Beverly nodded. "But the man that came by, he warned me. He told me that I shouldn't trust you." Her eyes wide with fear, she added, "That you weren't stable."

Alaina's heart pounded against her ribs. Was she already too late? "What man?"

"The FBI agent. He left me his card." Her fingers shaking, Beverly lifted a business card from the end table next to the couch.

Alaina took it from her. Agent Vincent Vonner. "He was here? When?"

"Last night."

She shivered with the knowledge that Beverly had already been found. "Was he alone?"

"No, there was another agent with him—some gray-haired guy. He didn't tell me his name. But Agent Vonner told me to call him if I needed anything." Beverly's eyes warmed with appreciation of Vonner's good looks, and she smiled. "And he promised that he would come right back."

Alone? With no witnesses? Maybe Trent's

suspicions about the agent were justified and not just the jealousy she'd suspected.

Alaina moved from the couch to the window, peering through the sheer lace curtains at the street outside the small house. The dark-colored sedan she'd noticed when she'd driven up was gone now. If it had been the federal protection that she'd promised the women, that she'd hoped it was, the agent wouldn't have left.

The car, and whoever had hid behind the tinted windows, was gone. For now...

But whoever he'd been, Alaina knew that he would come back.

To finish what he'd begun over thirty years ago.

He studied the silhouette at the window, behind the lacy curtain. He recognized the willowy figure. It was her—Audra Kooiyer. Or as she called herself now, Alaina Paulsen. She was here. To protect the other victim or to die with her?

But he didn't want to kill both women. Not anymore. Killing those old victims, stealing their hearts, gave him no satisfaction. As they had in their past lives, they proved poor substitutes for the real woman. For Audra...

She had been so beautiful with her pale skin and red hair. So passionate with her kisses, her caresses…

His body hardened, needing hers. But she had just left *his* arms.

The only woman he wanted to kill was her. She had to die.

Her and Trent Baines.

## Chapter 18

"I expected a federal agent to have better security than that flimsy lock," Trent mused as he stared down the sight on his gun to Vonner's dark gaze.

"What the hell do you want, Baines?" Water dripped from his black hair and ran down his face.

If the agent hadn't been in the shower, Trent probably wouldn't have gotten the jump on him. As it was, Vonner had been reaching for his gun, sitting in his holster, on the chipped porcelain sink, when Trent had burst through the bathroom door.

"I want the truth."

Vonner snorted his derision. "You? The way you blur the lines between fact and fiction? You're not interested in the truth. You're interested in sales, in stirring up interest in your books."

"What?"

"That's the only motive I could figure for your starting up the killing again. Of course, you could just be nuts." As if Trent didn't have a gun on him, Vonner reached for towels, wrapping one around his hips and rubbing another over his head and chest.

The bathroom was small, steam fogging the mirror. Moisture even beaded on the barrel of the gun Trent held steady on the guy. His vision blurred, not from the steam, but with confusion over Vonner's obvious truthfulness.

"You really think I'm the killer?" Trent asked, amazed that the guy seemed so certain. If Vonner had only been trying to hide his own guilt, he wouldn't have been so sincere.

"Convinced," the agent said matter-of-factly.

"I think it's you," Trent admitted.

Vonner laughed. "Yeah, right…" Then he met Trent's gaze and his laughter faded. "You're serious. Why the hell…? What reason would I have?"

"Maybe you're acting out. You're pissed because the woman you wanted rejected you, then chose someone else." That had been the Thief of Hearts' motive thirty years ago.

Vonner snorted his disbelief. "Alaina? We're talking about Alaina?"

"Isn't she why you got yourself assigned to this cold case?" Trent prodded him. "You wanted on it because she was working it?"

Vonner pushed a hand through his wet hair. "No. I didn't even know who Agent Paulsen was then. I didn't even know anyone was working that case. It sure as hell didn't seem like anyone was."

The agent's anger and resentment overwhelmed Trent again, the emotions so dark and intense. But Trent's brow furrowed in confusion. He didn't understand any of what the other man felt.

"Why did you want to work that case?" he asked. "Why does it mean so much to you?"

"None of your freakin' business," Vonner snapped. "You know you're in deep now, right? It was one thing for you and her to show up at a murder scene—that could have been the accident or coincidence you claimed it was. But this," he said, gesturing toward the gun Trent held on him, "is breaking and entering, threatening the life of a federal agent. You're going away, Baines."

That had been his plan. To take Alaina away, to bring her back to the fortress and keep her safe. But then he'd realized that wasn't the best way to keep her safe. The best way was to find the killer and stop him. His finger twitched where he held it along the barrel.

Vonner narrowed his eyes, studying the way Trent held the gun. "I've checked you out. Extensively," he admitted. "You're a college dropout. A recluse. And even though I looked and looked, I couldn't find any source you had in law enforcement. It actually seems like you've done very little research for your books."

"Yeah…" Trent conceded the veracity of the agent's claims.

"So where the hell did you learn that?"

"What?"

"The finger along the barrel," Vonner pointed out. "That's a cop's safety."

"Cop's safety? What the hell are you talking about?" And why? To distract Trent so that he could overpower him? He tensed, staying alert. However, nothing but curiosity emanated from Vonner now.

"Because police weapons don't have safeties, cops hold their finger along the barrel instead of the trigger," the agent explained. "Who taught you that?"

Trent shrugged. "I don't know…"

"I didn't find anyone, but you must have someone inside the department or the Bureau," Vonner said. "That's how you got so many of the details right in your books. It can't be Alaina. I found no connection between the two of you beyond when you met just a few days ago."

If only he knew how many years, how many lifetimes, their connection went back… But the agent had laughed at the idea of reincarnation.

"Graves denied it," Vonner persisted, "but is it the director?"

"He did work the case back then," Trent said, "with another detective."

Vonner snorted his disgust. "The guy that got burned out and took off? He was no cop."

"No," Trent agreed. "He was a fool." He sighed and lowered the gun. "And so am I. I thought it was you. I hoped it was you."

"Because of Alaina," Vonner said. He didn't reach for Trent's gun or his own. "If it's not me and it's not you, couldn't it be her?"

Trent shook his head. "You know it's not me?"

Vonner sighed. "I'll admit I wanted it to be you." He shook his head, as if disgusted with himself now. "But my gut tells me it's not."

"What about the director?"

"Could be," Vonner allowed. "I don't trust anyone, you know."

"Yeah." Trent didn't even trust himself. "The director said Rosenthal worked the murders, too."

"Rosenthal? The coroner?" Vonner chuckled. "I can't see him as a killer. At least, it would seem like he'd do a neater job of taking out the hearts, you know? Most people call coroners butchers, but I never figured Rosenthal that way.

'Course he is a fan of yours. So's the director."
Vonner snorted again. "Go figure…"

"I take it you're not a fan?"

"Hell, no. I question the sanity of anyone who
is—" His body tensed, and Trent felt his disgust
and resentment. "You glorified the killer. Now
that guy, whoever the hell he is, must be your
biggest fan."

Trent closed his eyes as the realization overwhelmed him. "Oh, my God…"

"You know who it is!" Vonner exclaimed.

"My biggest fan…"

The man's rage and hatred surged through
Trent. How had he not felt it? How had he not
known all these years? "We have to hurry."

He was going after Alaina.

Trent just hoped they wouldn't get to her—to
them—when he had the last time, in their past
life. When it was already too late…

Frustration tensed Alaina's muscles, so that she
moved stiffly as she walked into her apartment.
Her reflexes slow, she gasped at the shadow
looming in her living room before she reached
for her gun.

It wasn't Trent. As she'd walked up, she hadn't

felt him; she'd known before she'd opened the door that he'd be gone. But she hadn't expected anyone else.

"Ms. Paulsen," Dietrich said. "Mr. Baines asked me to wait for you to return."

"Where's Trent?" she asked, full of concern for the man she loved, regardless of who he might have been.

"He left already for the estate."

"I was supposed to go with him," she said. "This morning." The sun had only been up for a little while. "He left without me?"

Dietrich nodded. "It was too much for him to be in the city."

Of course. All the emotions. It was too exhausting for him to experience everyone else's feelings. She should have realized that; she should have gone back last night when he'd wanted to go.

"He had to leave," Dietrich said. "But he had me wait for you, so that I could bring you up to him."

"I can drive myself," she assured Trent's loyal assistant.

"No, that's not necessary," Dietrich insisted.

"He left me the helicopter, so I can get you to the estate—to him—quickly."

And no doubt so that his assistant/bodyguard could protect her from the danger he worried that she was in. "Then how did Trent get back?"

"Mr. Baines chartered a plane," Dietrich answered matter-of-factly.

Her lips twitched into a smile; no matter who he'd been, Trent Baines was a powerful man, the kind who was used to getting what he wanted when he wanted it. Like her. She smiled with affection for the man she loved. "Of course he did."

"He didn't want to drive or fly himself. He's writing," Dietrich explained. "He said he needed to finish the book. I know the publisher's been on him because he's missed his deadline. And Mr. Baines has never missed a deadline. I hope you understand."

Her smile widened. She did understand that not only was Dietrich Trent's employee but he was also his biggest fan. "Let me grab a bag and we can leave right away."

She needed to be with Trent. He wasn't just finishing a book; he was finishing their story.

Even now, from this distance, she could feel his fear and anxiety. She didn't want him to face the killer alone, even if it was only in his mind.

Dietrich glanced at her face as she descended the stairs from the helicopter pad on the roof of Trent Baines's fortress. Except it wasn't Trent's. He might have bought it in this life, but it didn't really belong to him.

It belonged to Dietrich; it was his heritage. His legacy. Just like the books were *his* story.

And *her*—she belonged to him, too. She just didn't realize it yet. But she realized Trent wasn't here. He saw the knowledge widen her eyes, saw her reach for her gun. But his hand was already there, pulling it from her hand as he jerked her up against him, trapping her between the cement wall of the stairwell and his hard body.

"What did you do to him?" she asked, her voice trembling with fear. Not for herself but for him—her lover. "Where's Trent?"

"I would worry less about Trent and more about yourself, Ms. Paulsen," he recommended.

"It's you," she said, her eyes glistening with tears and resignation as she shrank back against the wall. "It's always been you."

He laughed. "I didn't realize it myself...until I read his first book. Then everything clicked. All those feelings I had, all those violent memories. It all made sense. He made *me* make sense."

"Is that why you came to work for him?" she asked. Maybe she did understand him. "Because of what he'd written?"

"About me." Pride filled him.

"But..." Her throat moved as she swallowed hard. "But weren't you worried that he might catch on?"

"It wasn't easy," he admitted with frustration. "I could see that he felt things, that he felt all the emotions that other people felt. I had to be careful, so careful, around him." All those years of bottling up his emotions, of controlling his urges, so that Trent wouldn't figure out—too soon—who he'd been. Who he really was...

"So if it wasn't easy," Alaina asked, "why did you want to work for him?"

"We were friends, you know," he said. "All of us, in another life. We met in college. You and I were there for journalism, he for criminal justice."

"You remember everything?" she mused, her voice soft with awe.

He nodded. "And soon he would have, too."

"That's why you wanted to be around him," she said, her voice quavering now with the hint of tears that glistened in her wide eyes. "To stop him from remembering."

Dietrich realized that she must believe that he had already stopped Trent, that her lover was already dead.

Maybe that was how he should have handled it then and now. Maybe he should have killed his old friend first. But then he wouldn't have had the privilege of watching him suffer for all that he'd lost....

"No. I had to stick close to him because I knew *you* would eventually find him. I knew it was you when his editor called and said a female FBI agent was looking for him. I knew it was you. That was why I killed that first woman, because you'd started it all up again."

Her breath caught in an audible gasp and guilt rounded her eyes.

"Yeah, thanks for creating that website. It really helped me out," he taunted her.

"But why? You hadn't killed anyone yet. And you hadn't even met me. How could you know for sure that I was…that I'd been…"

"Audra. You're Audra." He laughed, letting to the surface all the bitterness that he'd harbored for two lifetimes. "You wouldn't leave him. You wouldn't stop loving him, even after I cut out your heart. It was supposed to be mine. You were always supposed to be mine."

She shook her head, and her blond hair swirled around her shoulders and a lock of it brushed across his jaw. He wrapped the pale strands around his finger. But in his mind, he saw the fire of her red hair; he saw the woman she used to be.

And he heard her voice when she said, "I loved him then and I love him now."

"You're going to make me do it again," he said, choking against the bitterness and regret. Of course he'd known even before they'd laid eyes on each other what would happen when Elijah and Audra met again. The same thing that had happened last time. Love at first sight. And he'd been dumped with an apologetic "I hope you understand, Ben. Please, let's all stay friends."

"You bitch," he cursed her, and his grip tightened on her hair until she winced. He shoved her back against the wall, away from him. "You're going to make me cut out your heart."

"It still won't belong to you," she taunted him. "I will always love him."

He struck her then, hard enough to crack her lip and send droplets of her blood across the wall of the stairwell. She only fell back a step; she didn't fall down. She didn't pass out. She was stronger this time.

When she lifted her leg to kick out, he raised the gun he'd taken from her and pressed the barrel to her temple. "Do you want to end it this quickly?" he asked. "I had so much more fun planned for us."

She shuddered in revulsion. "I know what you have planned. I remember…"

"You only know how it ended for you," he pointed out. "You don't know how the rest of it played out. You don't know what happened to me and Trent in the past life."

Her eyes widened. "Trent's still alive?"

He chuckled in anticipation of what was to come. "Just for now. But don't get your hopes up. Just like last time, he won't outlive you by much." He tilted his head, altering his plan a bit. "Actually, I think you won't outlive him by much, just enough so that this time you'll know exactly what will happen to him if you don't fall for the right man."

Her breath caught, then expelled in a shaky sigh. But it was apparent her fear was more for her lover than herself when she asked, "What are you going to do to him?"

"Shh…" he said, pressing his finger across her swollen lip, pushing hard enough that she winced again. But she didn't whimper or scream. Yet. "Don't worry. You'll know soon enough."

Her mouth moved against his finger, smearing blood across his skin. He pulled his hand away from her face and studied the bright red streak. And he remembered the last time her blood had run over his hands, when he'd held her heart in his palms.

"Tell me what happened last time," she persisted, "between you and Detective Kooiyer."

He shook his head, amused by her attempt to outwit him. "Nice try, but we're going to wait for Trent. And then you'll find out. I'll show you exactly what happened."

She licked the blood from her lip. "B-but... what if he doesn't come?"

He laughed at her ignorance. She knew so little of them all. "He'll come."

"Did you leave him a note?" she asked, her brow knitted with confusion. "How will he know?"

"I don't have to tell him a thing," Dietrich assured her. "He'll know that you're where you belong. With me."

And this time, when Eli tried to take her away, he'd be ready for him.

## Chapter 19

"How do you know for sure that he has her?" Vonner asked as Trent landed the FBI helicopter on the roof of the fortress, next to his, the one Dietrich had stolen from the airport hangar.

"He has her."

"But she could be with one of those women," Vonner said, "like the one who called to tell me that Alaina had been to see her."

Trent pulled off his headphones and vaulted out of the copter. As the engine he'd just shut off wound down, he shouted above the noise of the weakly whirring blades. "She's here."

"But she could be with one of those other women from that website," Vonner insisted as he followed him to the door to the stairs. "One of the women from that list you got going."

From the list he'd had Dietrich pull together for him. Guilt sickened him. How had he been such an unsuspecting fool? Again?

"She's here." He pointed to the droplets of blood on the wall of the stairwell. He smeared a trembling fingertip in it and streaked a jagged red line across the cement wall.

Vonner grimaced. "It's wet yet. But there's not much of it, just a few drops. She's still alive."

Rage gripped Trent. His own. "He hurt her...."

Vonner grabbed his arm and squeezed. "We don't know for sure that it's Alaina's. Hell, it could even be his blood. He could have cut himself."

"She's here," Trent insisted, sick of arguing with the dubious agent.

But the house was empty, Vonner's patience thinning as they searched the rooms. Trent closed his eyes, feeling Alaina's fear. She was close.

And she was alive. Yet. But not for long. Dietrich had waited another lifetime to end this. His patience wouldn't last much longer. Just as Trent could feel her fear, he could feel the killer's rage and madness.

"I don't get this," Vonner said. "I don't understand any of it." Yet he'd gone to the director for Trent. He'd gotten permission for Trent to use the FBI helicopter.

Maybe he'd known that if he hadn't, Trent would have found a way to take it, anyhow. He was that desperate. So desperate that he ran through the house, slamming open secret panels, searching every nook and cranny of the house he'd always thought too big.

"Dietrich being a sick, obsessed fan—that I can understand," Vonner said as he hurried after Trent. "Some people are just nuts."

"It's more than that," Trent insisted. On the way from Detroit to the U.P., he'd told Vonner everything—much to the man's astonishment and disbelief.

"But how can you and Alaina be so sure that this reincarnation thing is real?" he asked, as if he needed not only to understand but to believe, too.

"C'mon," Trent snapped, his impatience and frustration overwhelming him. "You read my books. You saw the scars on those women. And even this…" He gestured to how he held his gun. "You noticed this, my cop safety."

"So you're saying *you* were the detective?" Vonner asked as he sucked in an unsteady breath. "And who was Dietrich?"

"The reporter, Benjamin Lee." He remembered everything now, without even needing to write it down. Fear for Alaina's safety had brought it all rushing back. "Ben was Eli Kooiyer's friend from college. His family owned this property." Until Trent had bought it from a nephew of the reporter's.

"So you were all just drawn to one another?" he asked, the disbelief back.

"The book drew him to me. He was my biggest fan." Because Trent had unknowingly glorified what the monster had done, what he'd been.

"And the book drew Alaina, too. I get that," Vonner said as he followed Trent back to the two-story foyer. "But this place… Why would you be drawn to this place?"

An image flashed behind Trent's closed eyes. Rafters and blood. So much blood.

"I know…" Because it was where he had died. And where Dietrich no doubt intended to kill him again.

"Yeah, so why?" Vonner asked.

"You can keep searching the house. I'm going to check outside," he said. If only he'd checked the barn before. He wouldn't have spent so much of his life wondering what he'd been.…

"I saw the barn from the helicopter," Alaina said.

"You weren't even looking at the ground," Dietrich scoffed as he shoved her along the trail. "You were thinking only of him."

She stumbled, tripping over roots as briars tugged at her pants. Dietrich pushed her again, and she fell, then scrambled back to her feet.

"When Trent flew me down to Detroit the other day, I saw it then," she explained, fighting back her fear and panic so that she could figure out how to fight him, how to protect herself and Trent from the sadistic games Dietrich had planned for them.

"What did he say about it?" the madman demanded to know.

She shrugged. "Just that it was dilapidated. What makes you think he'll look for us here?"

His voice firm with conviction, he insisted, "He'll look."

"He had no reaction to seeing the barn," she shared. "It meant nothing to him."

"This property means something to him."

"An escape from his empathy," she agreed, wondering if Trent could feel her emotions now, if he was experiencing her fear and panic.

Was he still too far away? Or had Dietrich been telling the truth, that he'd heard the whirring blades of another helicopter? But how would Trent have procured another one so quickly? Of course, he was a powerful man used to getting what he wanted.

"This is just a place for him to lock himself away from feeling what everyone else feels."

Dietrich laughed but said nothing more until the barn came into view. The walls, made of fieldstone, looked as if they were about to crumble into dust, and the roof sagged, as if about to collapse or implode. "I wanted to fix up the barn," he said. "Do you know what he said?"

She shook her head, afraid to give him the wrong answer and get struck again. Her swollen lip throbbed in time with her racing pulse.

"He told me to have it torn down." His hand tightened around her arm, holding her near him as he jerked open the door. Rusty hinges creaked and groaned in protest but the door opened far enough for him to shove her through the opening. She tried to jerk away from him, but his hand tightened. Then his broad shoulders stuck between the door and jamb.

She tugged free of his painfully tight grasp, dropped to her hands and knees and scrambled away from him.

"There's no other way out," he warned her. "No other way but past me." The crack of wood echoed throughout the cavernous space as Dietrich broke through the door.

Her legs shaky with fear and adrenaline, Alaina regained her feet and ran. But the floor was as crumbling as the rest of the building. Missing boards opened holes to the dirt-filled cellar. She skirted the gaping areas, but boards broke beneath her weight. Her foot slipped through, trapping her.

Dietrich laughed. "I told you. You can't escape me, Audra."

She tugged, trying to free herself as he approached, his steps slow and measured as the boards trembled and creaked beneath his weight.

"You and I belong together," he insisted, his dark eyes gleaming with madness, glittering in the sunlight streaking through the missing boards of the roof. "If only you'd have realized that before. Maybe in our next life, you will…"

Tears burned Alaina's eyes as she struggled, slivers of wood slicing through the denim of her jeans to bite into her skin. Ignoring the pain, she shook her leg. Then more wood cracked and she fell to the ground below.

Breath left her lungs in an expulsion of air that stirred the dirt and cobwebs. Her chest burned, aching from the contact with the ground. At least it was only dirt, no rocks. Nothing else but spiders and cobwebs. And the rats of which Trent had spoken scurried around in the shadows cast by the boards that remained of the floor above.

Choking for breath, she turned her head and stared into the empty eye sockets of a skull. A scream burned her throat.

"I see you found Trent." Dietrich's deranged laughter echoed throughout the barn. "Actually, his name was Elijah back then. Elijah Kooiyer. I called him Eli."

Trent had been the detective, her husband. The man she'd betrayed.

"You were his friend," she said. She rolled onto her back and stared through the fresh hole to where Dietrich stood over her, her gun trained on her.

He gestured with the barrel to the other side of her. "And there I am."

She turned toward the other skeleton. "Who were you?"

"Benjamin Lee."

The name rang a bell; maybe she had seen one of the articles he'd written. Or maybe she remembered him from that other life. "The reporter."

He nodded. "Like you were going to be before you met and married Eli."

She turned back to the other skeleton. No more

than a few feet separated the two of them. "What happened?"

"Aren't you going to ask about yourself?" he taunted her. "You're here, too, you know."

She peered around the shadows and found a hole partially dug into the dirt foundation. A shovel, the wooden handle cracked and the blade rusty, lay on the ground next to it, as if the digger had been interrupted.

"I was going to bury you here, where I'd brought you when we were young, when you were still my girl," he said possessively. "Before you met Eli."

He sighed. "But he found us. And he wanted to take you away again. I couldn't let him do that."

While he trained the gun on her, he turned his head toward the creak of the door that signaled someone else's arrival. His voice shaking with fury and madness, Dietrich shouted, "I won't let you take her again, Eli!"

She rolled, just missing being hit by the bullets that slammed into the ground, kicking up dirt where she'd lain. In the protection of the shadows, she regained her feet and pressed herself against the stone wall. But the shooting stopped.

Despite the faint light, she found the ladder anchored to the fieldstone foundation, leading to the level above. The level where the man she loved and the man she feared would stage a duel over her. Again? Perhaps that was how Elijah and Ben had died just feet from each other.

She knew that Trent would follow through on his promise and that he would do whatever he had to in order to protect her this time. But like last time, she was the one who'd put herself—and him—in danger. She was the one who would get them both killed.

Shots rang out again but this time the bullets weren't directed into the basement. Dietrich fired her gun at Trent.

Even though she didn't know what she could do to help since she was unarmed, Alaina climbed the ladder and pushed aside the boards that blocked her from getting through. Splinters stung her fingers, burying deep into her skin.

She ignored that; she ignored everything but the pounding of her heart—and the pain and fear she felt. Trent's pain and fear. Had he been hit? She didn't care about herself; she cared only about him.

But then the pain was all hers as strong fingers grasped her hair and the blade of a knife pressed against her chest, over the old scar.

"I'm glad you're here, Eli. You can watch me this time," Dietrich taunted him, "as I cut out her heart."

# Chapter 20

Trent's hand shook as he gripped the gun, his finger on the trigger instead of the barrel. He was ready to shoot. And this time, with Dietrich out from behind the rusted body of an old tractor, he would have had a clear shot. But then Dietrich pressed the knife to Alaina's chest.

Blood oozed from her lip, streaking the dirt across her face. Even then, bruised and bleeding, she was beautiful. Love and fear for her life struck him as sharp as that knife pressing against her heart.

"You don't want to do this," Trent said, keeping

the big man in his sight. He still had the shot. But could he take it and drop the man before he plunged that knife into Alaina's heart?

Dietrich laughed. "I've been waiting to do this ever since I read your first book."

"But you hadn't killed anyone…"

"Until she found you," Dietrich admitted with a cough. "I knew who she was when your editor called. I was waiting for her to end this."

As Dietrich's voice weakened, Trent realized either he or Vonner had hit the man when they'd first burst into the barn and exchanged gunfire. He couldn't take his attention off the knife pressed to Alaina's chest, but he knew Vonner lay behind him, either dead or dying. He'd taken a couple of shots—shots that had been meant for Trent. But the federal agent had jumped in front of the bullets.

"Why did you wait all these years? Why not just kill *me?*" Trent asked, stalling the man. The more Dietrich bled, the more his grip on that knife weakened. "You've worked for me for almost ten years."

"It was never about you. Not this life. Not our

past. It was always about *her*." Dietrich pressed his lips to Alaina's forehead. "Audra…"

She shuddered as the tip of the knife penetrated her flesh. Blood oozed around the blade, staining her shirt.

Trent sucked in a breath, feeling pain. But it must have been his. Because if she felt any, it didn't show on her face. She didn't move, not even to wince or grimace.

"You're just going to watch me?" Dietrich taunted him. "You're just going to stand there while I cut out the heart of the woman you love?"

Trent had only one shot left; he'd made certain to leave one in the clip as they'd exchanged fire. Dietrich had emptied his and tossed away the gun. If only he hadn't had that damn knife…

Trent had seen it before, when they'd gone fishing. It was an old hunting knife. Probably an antique. At the least, thirty-some years old…

Dietrich had had the knife the whole time, the weapon with which he'd killed all those women before, the one with which he'd already once killed the woman Trent had loved.

"No," he finally answered the man. "I'm not just going to stand here."

"So kill me," Dietrich urged him. "Kill me, and I'll just come back again. You won't know when or as whom. But I'll be back. We *all* come back."

That was what Trent was afraid of…

"Eli had more guts," Dietrich taunted him. "When he finally figured it out, he ditched his FBI liaison. He came up here alone with one purpose. He wanted to make me suffer like I'd made his wife suffer. He wanted to kill me slowly, painfully, and he knew better than to bring along anyone who'd stop him."

That was the murderous rage Trent remembered; it had been his but for the man who'd killed the love of his life. Not for the woman who had been the love of his life.

"Do you know who he was?" Dietrich asked, nodding toward where Vonner lay on the floor near the door. The madman laughed again but this time he coughed and choked, as if blood gurgled in his throat and lungs. How badly had he been hit? Bad enough to die? And come back?

"Vonner's an FBI agent," Trent said. "He worked with Alaina."

"On this case. You didn't figure out why he was so attached to it? So obsessive about finding out what had happened to all the people involved?" Dietrich laughed and coughed and sputtered again. "He's your son."

Alaina gasped. And Trent felt her surprise and the flash of betrayal in her eyes. "We had a child...?" she asked, her voice quavering.

"Your lover didn't tell you that you left a son behind when you left him for me?" Dietrich taunted her now.

"I didn't leave him," Alaina insisted. "I wouldn't leave my husband." Her breath caught as her gaze moved from Trent to where Agent Vonner lay on the floor. "I wouldn't have... That's why you killed me. Because I wouldn't."

"That's why I have to kill you this time." Dietrich clicked his tongue against his teeth. "Because you fell for the wrong man again."

"I didn't fall," Alaina said, her gaze intent on Trent's face. "I have always loved him and I always will."

Trent felt Dietrich's rage and madness, but

before the man could plunge the knife deep, Alaina slammed her elbow into his stomach, then knocked the knife away from her chest. She wrestled free of his grasp but fell to her knees in front of him.

And Trent raised his gun.

"Kill me!" Dietrich shouted. "Kill me!" He started forward, reaching for Alaina. But before he could swing the knife toward her, Trent fired.

Curses rent the air, and Dietrich dropped to his knees, clutching his bloody hand that had taken the bullet. "You son of a bitch. You going to torture me again?"

"No, I remember now how that turned out last time," Trent reminded him. "And I have too much to live for. So do you. Prosecution. You're going to live a long, long life, my old friend, behind bars."

Alaina jerked Dietrich's arms behind him and slapped cuffs around his wrists. The director hadn't taken those away from her. She didn't know why she'd clipped them to her belt, except out of habit. As she grasped his bloody hand, the big man screamed out in pain.

"Are you all right?" Trent asked her.

Alaina pressed her free hand to her chest, where blood stained her shirt. But the wound was shallow. Just a scratch. The only pain she felt was Trent's—and Vonner's. Her son? "I'm fine."

She wanted to run to Trent, to throw her arms around him and hold him tight. But other memories tugged at her. Screaming in childbirth, a loving man stroking her hair, holding her hand as she brought their child into the world. Instead of running to Trent, she walked around him to where Vonner lay on the floor by the door.

"He pushed me out of the way," Trent said. "He took a bullet for me."

Alaina dropped to her knees next to the fallen agent. "I don't see any blood." She reached out, but before her fingers could touch Vonner's chest, he caught her hand. Shock and relief surged through her. "You're alive!"

He pressed his free hand over his heart, as if surprised himself. "Yeah…"

"H-how?" Dietrich, and Trent, had been so certain he was dead.

"Bulletproof vest," he murmured. "Still got

knocked on my ass, though." He rolled to his side and blinked, peering around her. "What happened? Did Baines kill him?"

"No," Trent said. "He's all yours." His breath shuddered out in an audible sigh of relief. "I'm not a killer."

"You sound as surprised as I am," Vonner said with a weak chuckle. "I also hear sirens."

"That backup you called," Trent reminded him.

Vonner admonished him. "The backup you wouldn't wait for."

"Not with Alaina's life at risk."

"But you risked yours," Alaina said, watching the banter between the men and wondering how so much had changed between them. She wondered, too, how they could be father and son....

Vonner got to his feet, swayed a bit, then regained his balance. "Okay, I'm okay," he assured them when Alaina and Trent both rushed forward. "Fine, just fine."

"You sure?" Trent asked, his eyes narrowed, his face white with shock.

Vonner nodded.

Then Trent pulled Dietrich to his feet and

pushed him toward the federal agent. "He's all yours."

Vonner dragged Dietrich toward the door but glanced back at Trent and Alaina, his brow furrowed with confusion. "I'll be back to question you two."

Alaina waited until they were alone, then she said, "I have questions, too."

"They can wait," Trent said as he pulled her into his arms. "I just want to hold you." He held her tight and shuddered.

His relief—and his love—filled her. She didn't need the words to know how he felt.

"I love you, too." Heedless of her swollen lip, she pressed her mouth to his. "I love you."

His fingers tangled in her hair as he held her head still, gentling the kiss. His breath sighed across her lips. "I was so afraid that I was going to lose you again."

"Never…"

Trent's fingers itched to get to the keyboard. He now knew exactly how to end the *Thief of Hearts* series forever. But Vonner paced his office, pushing a hand through his hair in a gesture familiar to Trent, as he did it himself.

"I thought you were both nuts," he admitted. "This reincarnation stuff just seems so far-fetched. But you both really lived before?"

Trent nodded, still unable to comprehend that this man was his son. And he wasn't the only one struggling with the reality of their new lives.

"And him, too? The killer?" Vonner's throat rippled as he swallowed hard.

"He was the reporter—the friend of Detective Kooiyer's," Trent explained.

"And you were Kooiyer." He lifted his gaze to Alaina, where she stood beside Trent. "And you were his wife." The man's dark eyes glistened. "It seems so unbelievable. But you all know so much—things that I don't even know, and I was alive back then."

"You were only three," Alaina said, tears streaming down her face and dripping from her chin. "You were only three when we died."

Vonner rubbed his hand over his face. "The people at the home said I kept waiting for my parents to come back and get me, that I didn't believe they weren't coming back for me."

"The home?"

"I grew up in an orphanage." He sighed. "Well,

I lived there for a while but I finally got adopted when I was twelve. That was when my name changed. From Benjamin Kooiyer to Vincent Vonner."

"Nine years in an orphanage." The disgust for the man he'd once been filled Trent again. He'd been such a fool hell-bent on revenge when he'd had a son depending on him, a son he'd named for the man who'd betrayed him. Benjamin…

"The orphanage was a strange place," Vonner said with a chuckle. "In an old church. It actually wasn't that bad."

"I'm sorry," Alaina said. "I'm so sorry…"

"Hey, none of it's your fault." The steady thumping of helicopter blades drew Vonner's attention; he lifted his gaze to the ceiling of the den. "I gotta go. I'm not sure how to deal with this, you know. I'm older than you guys are. I don't know…"

"We'll figure it out," Trent promised, his arm around Alaina. "We'll figure it out." But then he released her. "I'm going to walk him up to the roof. Why don't you go lie down?" he suggested.

She looked as if she wanted to protest, but

exhaustion overcame her resistance. And she reluctantly walked away from them.

"And if I can't deal?" Vonner asked after Alaina disappeared up the hidden stairwell. "If it's easier for me to have nothing to do with you guys?"

"We'll deal with that, too," Trent assured him as he glanced toward the stairwell.

"I mean…" Vonner's breath shuddered out and he shrugged. "Hell, you know, it's too weird."

"I know," Trent agreed. "I struggled for years to figure out what the hell was real and what was just my imagination."

Vonner nodded. "Yeah, you get it."

"There's something I don't get," Trent admitted. "How you survived getting shot, repeatedly, back at the barn. You jumped in front of those bullets. You took more than one."

"Told you, bulletproof vest." He thumped his chest, where a bullet-size hole had torn through the fabric of his suit jacket and the shirt beneath it.

"I was there when you got dressed," Trent reminded him. "You aren't wearing a bulletproof vest. What's with you? Are you some kind of superhero?"

"Some kind," Vonner said with a grin. "Like I told you, that old church was one strange place. The kids that spent a lot of time there…we're a little bit different from everyone else."

"Indestructible?" Trent asked.

Vonner shrugged. "Untouchable." He chuckled. "Hell, I guess if I can accept that I can accept that you and Alaina are the reincarnated souls of my dead parents." His breath shuddered out in a ragged sigh. "Now I gotta deal with their murderer."

"I'd tell you to be careful," Trent said, "but somehow I don't think I need to worry about you."

Alaina stood in the shower, washing off the dirt from the barn and her blood and the killer's touch. She scrubbed her skin and shampooed her hair, trying to get rid of the past—at least the part of it that made her feel dirty.

Through the glass-block walls of the shower, she glimpsed a shadow. But no fear quickened her pulse. She felt only relief. And love.

Then Trent stepped under the water with her.

He wrapped his arms around her and pulled her back against his chest.

"Will he be okay?" she asked, her heart aching as she thought of their son growing up alone in an orphanage, thinking his parents had left him there, forgotten him. Rejected him, just as her father had rejected her. She felt his pain as she remembered her own.

"Oh, yeah, he'll be fine," Trent assured her with a soft chuckle of admiration for the man he'd once suspected of being the killer.

She tilted her head back, trying to meet his gaze. "What about us?"

"He took our statements," Trent said, misunderstanding her question, maybe deliberately. "Hell, Dietrich confessed all."

"Like anyone will believe he was the killer from thirty years ago when he's only twenty-nine." At least her son believed, even if he struggled to accept, that they were the reincarnated souls of his parents.

"They've got the killer," he reminded her. "They found his skeleton in the basement of the barn and the murder weapon, along with the chest of hearts that Dietrich found there."

"Eli caught the killer," she said. "His skeleton was there, too." As was hers…in that uncovered hole in the cellar.

"Too bad he hadn't brought him to justice instead of doling out his own," Trent said with a heavy sigh of guilt. "Then his son wouldn't have had to grow up alone."

"At least Vonner has their remains now," she said, her breath catching with regret. "He can bury them and have some closure. And so can the families of those other victims."

"And the new victims will have justice, too," Trent said. "Dietrich's DNA was found at the last two crime scenes. Vonner's closed all the Thief of Hearts cases. Old and new."

Pride filled Alaina. "Maybe he'll get a promotion."

"The promotion and the credit should really be yours," Trent said.

She shook her head. "No. I was stupid. I made so many mistakes." In this life and her past one. "And everyone at the Bureau thinks I'm crazy now."

"We can get you a lawyer to protest your

firing. But you probably won't get your job back," he agreed, pressing his lips to her shoulder.

Goose bumps rose on her skin even though the water remained hot. "That's okay. I think the only reason I really went into law enforcement was because I wanted to find out the truth. I wanted to know about this scar." She pressed her fingers to the mark over her heart; now there was a fresh scratch over the faded scar.

Trent leaned over and replaced her fingers with his lips, kissing the sensitive skin. "I would have shot him…"

"But you're not a killer," she said.

"I was," he admitted, and she felt his guilt.

She had her own.

"And I betrayed you," she reminded him. "In that other life. Can you ever forgive me? Can you ever trust me?"

His breath shuddered out, warm against her skin. "I made so many mistakes, too. I didn't pay you enough attention. I didn't protect you. I was such a fool.…"

"We were both fools," she agreed, then voiced her greatest fear, one she knew he felt, too. "So can we forgive ourselves and start new?"

"We lived before," he said, "but we're not really those people anymore. Our souls are older and wiser now. We won't make the same mistakes we did last time."

"No, we won't," she promised. "We won't lose each other again." Alaina turned in his arms and linked hers around his neck. She pressed her naked body against his, wet skin sliding over wet skin.

His hands trembling slightly, Trent ran them up and down her back. Then he cupped her buttocks and lifted her. She wrapped her legs around his waist, feeling his erection push against her. She reached between them, sliding her thumb over the pulsing tip of him before she guided him inside her. Emotions crashed over them as they made love with an explosive passion.

Trent thrust in and out of her and lowered his head, loving her breasts with his mouth, teasing the aching nipples with the tip of his tongue.

Pressure built inside Alaina, insistent and fierce. When she thought she could stand it no longer, an orgasm slammed through her, more intense than she'd ever felt, and she screamed his name. His hands tightened on her butt as he tensed and groaned. Then with one final thrust he came. Heat pulsed inside Alaina as he filled her.

Her legs, weak from desire and exhaustion, trembled as she regained her feet. He washed her again, quickly, then wrapped her in a towel and carried her to the bed, every gesture an expression of the love she felt in his touch and in his heart.

"What will you do," he asked as he laid her onto the sheets, "if you're not going to be able to work for the Bureau anymore?"

"Afraid I'm going to disrupt your writing?" she teased as she tugged him down beside her.

"I do have a book to finish," he said with a sigh as he settled into the bed with her still wrapped in his arms, pressed tight against his heart. "But then the series is over after that."

"Will you quit writing?" she asked, tilting her face to his.

"No," he said, then grinned with an excitement that sparkled like the love in his green eyes. "I have an idea for a new series about a superhero FBI agent."

"Will I be in your way if I stay up here?"

Alaina wondered, remembering what Dietrich had claimed about how Trent wrote, how he wanted no interruptions.

Trent's hand stroked along her side, as if he'd felt and wanted to soothe her doubts. "You would never be in my way. And no matter where we are, we will always be together," he vowed. "As soon as we can get a license, I intend to make you my wife again."

"From the moment I met you, I felt as though I already was," she admitted. "I feel like I am your wife."

"You are," he said, and leaned forward to brush his mouth across hers, taking care of her swollen lip. "But I'd still like to make it official in this life."

"Okay," she agreed. "I can handle that." And hopefully Vince could handle attending their wedding. She wanted him there.

As if he could read her mind as well as her emotions, Trent assured her, "He'll come around. You'll see. He won't find it as hard to accept us as you fear."

"I hope he can deal with it."

"Will you be all right living here?" he asked. "We don't have to stay, especially after—"

"You can't be in the city around all those emotions. And I actually like it up here," she admitted with a smile. "I think it's going to be a great place to raise all the babies I want to have with you."

"Really?"

"Sounds horribly old-fashioned, doesn't it?" she realized with a laugh. "But I got cheated last time. I got robbed of being a mom. I want to do it right this time. I want to be a good wife and a good mother. I want to spend the rest of my life loving you."

"I will love you for the rest of this life and the next," Trent promised. "And the next and the next one after that…"

She pressed her mouth against his and murmured, "Forever…"

\* \* \* \* \*

# nocturne™

## COMING NEXT MONTH

### Available June 28, 2011

**#115 VACATION WITH A VAMPIRE...
AND OTHER IMMORTALS**
Maggie Shayne and Maureen Child

**#116 NIGHTWALKER**
*The Nightwalkers*
Connie Hall

You can find more information on upcoming
Harlequin® titles, free excerpts and more at
**www.HarlequinInsideRomance.com.**

# REQUEST YOUR FREE BOOKS!

## 2 FREE NOVELS PLUS 2 FREE GIFTS!

# nocturne™

**Dramatic and Sensual Tales of Paranormal Romance.**

**YES!** Please send me 2 FREE Harlequin® Nocturne™ novels and my 2 FREE gifts (gifts are worth about $10). After receiving them, if I don't wish to receive any more books, I can return the shipping statement marked "cancel." If I don't cancel, I will receive 4 brand-new novels every other month and be billed just $4.47 per book in the U.S. or $4.99 per book in Canada. That's a saving of at least 15% off the cover price! It's quite a bargain! Shipping and handling is just 50¢ per book in the U.S. and 75¢ per book in Canada.* I understand that accepting the 2 free books and gifts places me under no obligation to buy anything. I can always return a shipment and cancel at any time. Even if I never buy another book, the two free books and gifts are mine to keep forever.

238/338 HDN FC5T

| | |
|---|---|
| Name | (PLEASE PRINT) |
| Address | Apt. # |
| City | State/Prov. | Zip/Postal Code |

Signature (if under 18, a parent or guardian must sign)

Mail to the **Reader Service:**
**IN U.S.A.:** P.O. Box 1867, Buffalo, NY 14240-1867
**IN CANADA:** P.O. Box 609, Fort Erie, Ontario L2A 5X3

Not valid for current subscribers to Harlequin Nocturne books.

**Want to try two free books from another line?**
Call 1-800-873-8635 or visit www.ReaderService.com.

* Terms and prices subject to change without notice. Prices do not include applicable taxes. Sales tax applicable in N.Y. Canadian residents will be charged applicable taxes. Offer not valid in Quebec. This offer is limited to one order per household. All orders subject to credit approval. Credit or debit balances in a customer's account(s) may be offset by any other outstanding balance owed by or to the customer. Please allow 4 to 6 weeks for delivery. Offer available while quantities last.

**Your Privacy**—The Reader Service is committed to protecting your privacy. Our Privacy Policy is available online at www.ReaderService.com or upon request from the Reader Service.

We make a portion of our mailing list available to reputable third parties that offer products we believe may interest you. If you prefer that we not exchange your name with third parties, or if you wish to clarify or modify your communication preferences, please visit us at www.ReaderService.com/consumerchoice or write to us at Reader Service Preference Service, P.O. Box 9062, Buffalo, NY 14269. Include your complete name and address.

USA TODAY *bestselling author B.J. Daniels takes you on a trip to Whitehorse, Montana, and the Chisholm Cattle Company.*

*RUSTLED*

*Available July 2011 from Harlequin Intrigue.*

As the dust settled, Dawson got his first good look at the rustler. A pair of big Montana sky-blue eyes glared up at him from a face framed by blond curls.

A woman rustler?

"You have to let me go," she hollered as the roar of the stampeding cattle died off in the distance.

"So you can finish stealing my cattle? I don't think so." Dawson jerked the woman to her feet.

She reached for the gun strapped to her hip hidden under her long barn jacket.

He grabbed the weapon before she could, his eyes narrowing as he assessed her. "How many others are there?" he demanded, grabbing a fistful of her jacket. "I think you'd better start talking before I tear into you."

She tried to fight him off, but he was on to her tricks and pinned her to the ground. He was suddenly aware of the soft curves beneath the jean jacket she wore under her coat.

"You have to listen to me." She ground out the words from between her gritted teeth. "You have to let me go. If you don't they will come back for me and they will kill you. There are too many of them for you to fight off alone. You won't stand a chance and I don't want your blood on my hands."

"I'm touched by your concern for me. Especially after you just tried to pull a gun on me."

"I wasn't going to shoot you."

Dawson hauled her to her feet and walked her the rest of the way to his horse. Reaching into his saddlebag, he pulled out a length of rope.

"You can't tie me up."

He pulled her hands behind her back and began to tie her wrists together.

"If you let me go, I can keep them from coming back," she said. "You have my word." She let out an unladylike curse. "I'm just trying to save your sorry neck."

"And I'm just going after my cattle."

"Don't you mean your boss's cattle?"

"Those cattle are mine."

"*You're* a Chisholm?"

"Dawson Chisholm. And you are…?"

"Everyone calls me Jinx."

He chuckled. "I can see why."

*Bronco busting, falling in love…it's all in a day's work.*
*Look for the rest of their story in*

**RUSTLED**

*Available July 2011 from Harlequin Intrigue*
*wherever books are sold.*